SALLEY VICKERS is th‍‍ng
the bestselling *Miss* ‍‍‍‍‍‍‍‍‍‍‍‍‍‍‍‍‍‍‍‍‍‍ *he
Number 3, Mr Golig*‍‍‍‍‍‍‍‍‍‍‍‍‍‍‍‍‍‍‍‍ *of
You* and, most recentl‍‍‍‍‍*, Dancing Backwards*. She has
worked as a dancer, an artist's model, a university teacher
of literature and a psychoanalyst. She now writes full-
time and lives and works in London and Cambridge.

From the reviews of *Aphrodite's Hat*:

'A box of delights . . . the emotional and technical range
of this collection is both impressive and delightfully
disorienting . . . Frank O'Connor famously said that it
was possible for a bad writer to write a good novel,
but only a really good writer could write a decent short
story. Vickers's first collection proves beyond doubt that
she's a really good writer'
FRANK COTTRELL BOYCE, *Guardian*

'Vickers's observant eye ensures her stories are psychologi-
cally rich . . . With this collection, Vickers proves herself a
formidable and astute chronicler of the psychology of love'
LUCY SCHOLES, *Sunday Times*

'She is an engaging writer, and this collection of stories
sparkles with dry wit and shrewd insights'
Mail on Sunday

'Wise, bittersweet tales which orbit the theme of love . . .
Vickers has carved a niche in contemporary fiction for
books which are thoughtful yet readable, romantic yet
modern, rich with references to art and poetry, full of
the sensitive observations of one schooled in the human
condition twice over: in literature and in psychoanalysis'
SUSAN MANSFIELD, *Scotsman*

By the same author

Miss Garnet's Angel
Instances of the Number 3
Mr Golightly's Holiday
The Other Side of You
Where Three Roads Meet
Dancing Backwards

SALLEY VICKERS

Aphrodite's Hat

FOURTH ESTATE · London

Fourth Estate
An imprint of HarperCollins*Publishers*
77–85 Fulham Palace Road
Hammersmith
London W6 8JB

This Fourth Estate paperback edition published 2011
1

First published in Great Britain by Fourth Estate in 2010

A catalogue record for this book is available from the British Library

ISBN 978-0-00-737106-8

Set in Sabon by
Palimpsest Book Production Ltd,
Falkirk, Stirlingshire

AUTHOR'S NOTE

There are novelists and there are short story writers and there are those who try their hands at both. Although I am primarily a novelist, I take comfort from the fact that two of my very favourite short stories, 'The Dead' by James Joyce and 'The Eternal Moment' by E.M. Forster, were written by people who were pre-eminently novelists. In fact, I wrote my first short story, 'The Dragon's Bones', which is included in this collection, as a thank you to a great novelist but also a great short story writer, Penelope Fitzgerald, whose generous comments about my first novel, *Miss Garnet's Angel*, helped much towards the book's success. I was particularly grateful not only because I was an unknown writer but also because she was, and remains, one of my own top favourite writers. I treasure the postcards which she wrote to me over *Miss Garnet* but most especially the card she wrote to thank me for 'The Dragon's Bones': 'How lucky that you can do these. I find them so hard.'

That the past mistress of short stories should write this to me, an absolute beginner, was humbling. Very soon after writing this card Penelope Fitzgerald died and within a few months one of my other favourite authors, William Maxwell, had died too. It was one of those synchronicities that both wrote so convincingly of that, according to her daughters, Penelope Fitzgerald was reading Maxwell in the days before she died. Maxwell was a brilliant editor as well as a fine writer and in his role as literary editor of the *New Yorker*, he edited some of the stories which have influenced my own. These were by Sylvia Townsend Warner, who, like Maxwell, is not known nowadays as well as she should be. I have borrowed from her the notion that only lowly fairies fly.

Finally, writers are very sensitive to the atmosphere in which they write. Over the past years, I have been enormously helped by the kindness of my friend and former colleague, Dr Anthony Stevens, who, over the years I have been writing, has allowed me to visit his lovely Corfu home and write there in peace. At least two of these stories, and large parts of many of my novels, were written in this generative environment. The book is dedicated to him and to Corfu.

CONTENTS

MRS RADINSKY

'And what,' asked Mr Pullen, nervously shuffling his papers together on his knees, 'is to be done about Mrs Radinsky?'

It was the end-of-year meeting of Chesterton Court's Residents' Association and thanks to Mr Pullen's patient steering they had arrived finally – and thankfully, thought Clare Trevellyan – at 'Any Other Business'.

The atmosphere in Mr Pullen's cramped flat – where in deference to his role as chair the residents' meetings were always held – became uneasy. Mr and Mrs Hampshire, who, by virtue of their owning two of the penthouse flats, were accorded double voting powers, started forward on the perilously fragile chairs provided by Mr Pullen. Don Parsons, who had been hoping to get away sharpish, glanced anxiously across at his neighbour Susan Macclesfield and, catching her eye, sighed audibly. Other residents, who had been frankly dragooned into coming, shifted irritably, keen to get back to addressing their late Christmas cards.

Mr Pullen retrieved his glasses from the pocket of his cardigan and studied the past minutes as if refreshing his memory over what had been agreed when the topic of Mrs Radinsky last arose. This was purely a delaying tactic. He recollected all too well. And knew who would be asked to bear the lion's share of responsibility in dealing with her.

Chesterton Court had not always been the salubrious establishment it now was. As with so many formerly rough areas in London, it had 'come up'. The elegant white-stuccoed building, now boasting a live-in caretaker and a well-maintained garden, was once the shabby quarters of a housing association. Every previous occupant had long departed, except Mrs Radinsky.

Mrs Radinsky lived on the top floor, in number thirty-seven, in what was now described as a 'penthouse studio'. Nobody knew the precise age of the occupant, but it was guessed she must be in her seventies. This did not stand in the way of Mrs Radinsky's pursuit of her professional activities. In the past, no one at Chesterton Court had cared, or even noticed, that numbers of gentlemen callers regularly made their way, in those days up several flights of stone stairs, to Mrs Radinsky's flat, where they stayed, perhaps an hour, before letting themselves discreetly out again.

The procession of callers had not with time abated. If anything, numbers had swelled. Men of all ages, some surprisingly young, made their way, by means of the newly installed lift, to the sixth floor and, after a suitable lapse of time, down again.

Some of these visitors were seen carrying bottles of gin or vodka. This in itself would not perhaps have aroused hostility were it not for the fact that quantities of empty bottles were found, regularly, piled outside the waste area with no effort made to dispose of them in the environmental bins. Mrs Hampshire claimed to have stumbled on one when returning from a performance of *Swan Lake* and had given herself a nasty cut, said to have turned septic. She was now kicking herself that she had allowed the wearing of conspicuous plasters, which had been kept up for several weeks, to lapse that evening, forgetting that the topic of Mrs Radinsky was likely to come up at the residents' meeting.

She made up for this by rubbing her ankle vigorously while at the same time voicing an opinion. 'We must get the council in. She is breaking the law.'

'Technically not,' said Mr Pullen, who had once had some legal training and had paid for it ever since by getting lumbered with this sort of job. 'The garden area is ours so she is not infringing any actual, er, law.'

'My cleaner says there are rats,' retorted Mrs Hampshire, refusing to be sidetracked by reason.

'Rats?' Clive Butterworth looked alarmed. He was a tall young man, with a tendency to nervous rashes and a pathological horror of rats. So serious was this condition that he had abandoned a first degree in Eng. Lit. for one in Environmental Studies after he was asked to address a seminar on *1984*.

'Rats,' repeated Mrs Hampshire with ominous firmness, sensing she had collared an ally.

'Rats are health and safety,' Mr Pullen explained. 'They are not, sadly, illegal.' He smiled at his little attempt at lightening the tone but, getting no response, quickly readjusted his expression to one of grave concern.

'What is it she does, anyway?' asked Clare Trevellyan, who was slim and pretty, with the easy-going kindness of the young, before time has had too much of a go at them. She was not strictly a resident at all but had come along on behalf of her cousin, Hetty, whose flat Clare was using while Hetty, single-handed, was sailing round the world.

An atmosphere, largely emanating from Mrs Hampshire, at once fell upon the room. Really, if this young interloper didn't know . . .!

'But we don't know, do we?' Clare Trevellyan persisted, responding to the unstated reproach. 'I mean she can't, really, at her age still be on the game.'

Clive Butterworth giggled and Mrs Hampshire shot him a warning look which suggested that she would not tolerate any backsliding.

'Whatever she is up to,' she said, giving the phrase sinister emphasis, 'it is a condition of the lease that the apartments are not used as places of work.'

This was a mistake. Everybody knew that any number of the residents carried out small self-employed businesses and relied on each other for assistance with computer shut-downs, blocked drains, late tax returns and Feng Shui. The mood of the room began to disassociate itself from Mrs Hampshire and sensing this she afforded Clive Butterworth a fickle smile.

But Clive, unwilling to be thought a wimp by Clare Trevellyan, had in the blink of an eye transferred his allegiance. 'In that case, as I understand it, half the building would be asked to leave.'

'In any event,' said Mr Pullen, he hoped placatingly, 'Mrs Radinsky is not a leaseholder. As you know, she is a long-term tenant. It is, I'm afraid, up to us to persuade the council that it is time for her to be re-housed.'

'What do you suppose she does do, though?' Clive asked Clare. As the youngest members of the meeting, they had elected to take the stairs, leaving the others to pack themselves by turns into the inconveniently small lift. Clive, who was behind Clare, observed her ankles with pleasure as she ran down the steps.

'Don't know,' Clare said over her shoulder. 'And don't care. I just didn't like that dreadful creature getting at the poor old duck.'

'I don't know that "duck" describes her,' said Clive. He was a quiet young man but he noticed things. He had noticed Mrs Radinsky's callers. It was hard to know what to make of them, but they appeared to be men of the world.

A few days later, he bumped into the object of these calls herself. Mrs Radinsky, carting several bulky bags, was getting into the lift. Clive held the door for her and then, not wanting to seem to avoid her – though for the sake of fitness it was his habit to take the stairs – followed her in.

'Bless you, dear,' Mrs Radinsky said.

She was a small woman, with remarkably black hair, well-carmined lips and bright hazel eyes. The eyes put Clive in mind of a bird's. She smelled of something powdery, which might have been marguerite but was in fact lily-of-the valley and reminded Clive of his grandmother. She was wearing red suede gloves, what appeared to be a man's tweed coat, cut down, and a fluffy red scarf. Nothing about her, unless you counted the lipstick, looked even faintly racy.

The lift took them to the top floor and again Clive held open the door. 'Thank you, dear,' said Mrs Radinsky. 'Come in and have a glass of something, if you like.'

Clive hesitated. There was the question of the rats. His curiosity was not so strong that it outreached his timidity. But then the thought of telling Clare Trevellyan that he had penetrated number thirty-seven galvanised him.

'OK,' he said. 'Thank you.'

Mrs Radinsky's flat like Mrs Radinsky was small and dark with a preponderance of red. Fringed lampshades glowed hospitably crimson against a deep flock paper of a kind which Clive had only seen previously in the less upmarket type of Indian restaurant. The flock was almost invisible behind a crowd of pictures of a catholic range of subjects: two elephants giving a third a shower, some seductively ill-clad mermaids disporting themselves on rocks, a yoked horse standing patiently beneath a spreading oak, a lady in a pale blue crinoline squinting at a man in a frock coat.

On the crammed sideboard were a couple of ships in bottles. Noticing the direction of her guest's gaze, Mrs Radinsky said, 'My father was a naval man.' She indicated that Clive should sit down on a peach velour sofa, well ballasted with cushions, while she disappeared into the kitchen from where she could be heard whistling while unpacking bags.

'Sherry?' she called suddenly. 'Or something stronger?'

Clive, renouncing the idea of saying he would truly rather have tea, plumped for sherry.

'I only have the dry.'

'Dry's fine, thanks.'

'So what do you do?' asked Mrs Radinsky, presenting him with a cut-glass tumblerful of pale sherry and a china plate of sponge fingers.

Clive explained that he was training to be a surveyor.

'That's nice,' said Mrs Radinsky. With her coat and scarf off she looked younger. 'One of my gentlemen's a surveyor.' She looked at Clive with her bright bird's eyes. It was hard to say if it was knowingness or innocence in them.

Thinking of Clare Trevellyan, Clive took a plunge. 'Gentlemen?'

'My clients,' said Mrs Radinsky peaceably. She leant across him, took a sponge finger and dipped it into his glass of sherry. She herself was drinking nothing. 'They come to consult.'

In spite of Clare Trevellyan's ankles Clive couldn't find it in him to ask what the consultations consisted of. But here, surprisingly, his hostess helped out.

'Horoscopes,' she explained. 'That and the tarot and a bit of mediuming, though I'm sick to death of that.'

'But why only gentlemen?' Clive burst out.

Mrs Radinsky laughed. 'Gets them going here,' she said, nodding her head. 'It's my bit of fun. They think I'm a tart, see?' She pulled an impenetrable face and got up and went out of the room, returning with a manila file.

'I've got all the correspondence here. One of my gentlemen's in the council. He keeps an eye out. Sees we don't go too far. But there's nothing they can say. I'm not breaking the law. I don't charge, see? Me on the game? Chance would be a fine thing! Want their heads examining. Have another finger?'

'No, thanks,' said Clive, who hadn't touched the plate. He extracted a crumb from the sherry, hoping it didn't seem impolite. 'Why do your gentlemen come?'

'Love, mainly. They've had a love problem and someone tells them, "Go to Rita." I've a name. Then they get used to coming, just to talk. Everyone's got troubles and I listen to them. It's not the stars, really, you know, that tells me things. It's knowing how to look. For instance, you're in love. I saw it in your face. That's why I asked you in. When's your birthday?'

'Next week,' Clive said. 'December the twenty-second.'

'Ah, Christmas boy. They either turn out easy-going or resentful. You're the first sort, I can tell. Capricorn. Let's see . . . '76?'

'1977, actually.'

'Time of birth – not that it matters, but we always ask.'

'I don't know,' said Clive. 'Morning, I think. My mother said I arrived in time for breakfast.'

Mrs Radinsky closed her eyes, fluttered the lids a trifle alarmingly and then opened them and took another sponge finger. 'Sure you won't have one? Don't blame you. They're old as buggery. My judge brought them. Lord knows how long he'd had them. Your beloved's a Gemini, born 1984. They can be slippery, Geminis, but yours'll be all right.'

'How do you know?' Picturing Clare's dark blonde hair he didn't even question that she did.

'Instinct. You came in here, didn't you? That says a lot. Not many would. I had that Mr Pullen at my door last week. Pissing in his pants with embarrassment. "Oh, Mrs Radinsky it's about them bottles." They're not mine, you know.'

'No?'

Mrs Radinsky pulled another face. 'Think my gentlemen wouldn't take mine away?'

'Whose are they?' Of course she would know.

'Ah,' said Mrs Radinsky. 'I'm not saying. Not unless I have to. I'll go so far as to say it's a Virgo. You can't trust Virgos. They come across all goody-two-shoes but they're vicious underneath.'

The following week it was the residents' Christmas party, held, to accommodate the numbers, they graciously suggested, in the Hampshires' double penthouse. The view across London from both sides of the flat was, everyone agreed, quite superb. The pale walls were hung with discreetly lit modern paintings, the furniture was Conran, the wooden floors maple, the rugs principally white. Yes, Mrs Hampshire agreed with Susan Macclesfield, it was a trouble to keep them so spotless but then she was like that. It was in her stars. Nothing, Clive thought, as he turned away, with an upbeat of his heart as Clare Trevellyan entered the crowded room, could be less like the friendly fug of Mrs Radinsky's flat, which, he suddenly recognised, must be just the other side of the wall.

'Hi,' said Clare. She was dressed in a grey angora cardigan, a short black skirt and little ankle boots.

'Oh, hi.'

'How are you?'

Clive started to say he was all right and then said instead, 'I went to see Mrs Radinsky. Or rather she asked me in.'

'Well done you!'

'She's nice.'

'Good.'

'Not on the game at all. The idea's preposterous.' Clive had a hunch Clare would respond to this word.

'What is she then? Who are the callers?'

'When's your birthday?' Clive asked.

'June the tenth. Why?'

'Is that Gemini?'

'Yes.'

'And how old are you?'

'Twenty-six,' said Clare. 'What is this? A Spanish Inquisition?'

'Will you marry me?' Clive asked. 'I'm twenty-nine tomorrow, by the way.'

Clare said she thought she might but she had better sit down first.

Later, in bed, he said, 'You know, the Hampshires' flat is right next to Mrs Radinsky's in the next block?'

'So?'

'So I'm a surveyor, or will be. Old Hampshire's been sucking up to me since the meeting. Tried to find out what would be involved in extending their flat laterally.'

'Ah.'

'I think she's pretty safe, though. Rita.'

'Rita now, is it? I'll have to watch her, given what we are so reliably told about her!'

Clive patted Clare's bottom appreciatively. 'She'll like you. She saw you.'

'Saw me?'

But he had heard something. 'Hang on. There's a hell of a noise outside.'

They got up and, together relishing their nakedness in the December cold, stared out into the wintry darkness. A figure over by the bins straightened up and looked furtively about. Clive opened the window.

'Oh, Mrs Hampshire,' he shouted down. 'What a lovely party. We did enjoy ourselves. But we should have helped with all those bottles, instead of leaving them to you.'

JOIN ME FOR CHRISTMAS

Emily had met Lionel after many years managing on her own. For those who are not temperamentally suited to solitude, living alone feels not so much a trial as a waste. Emily's first husband, a physicist, had gone to America to deliver a lecture and had never returned. Emily was a little put out when, at a later date, she met the cause of his decampment. 'Dumpy, with red-veined cheeks', was how she described the new wife to her friend Deb. Emily herself was slight and on the whole did not forget her makeup. 'Perhaps he likes them with a bit more flesh,' Deb had, not too tactfully, replied.

While the children were small, Emily had coped with the life of a single parent, sometimes with a touch of despair, sometimes almost breezily. But when her younger daughter, Kate, left to study drama at Bristol University, Emily found herself crying into a brushed cotton nightdress – the one with koala bears on it which Kate had rejected as unsuitable for college wear. Emily knew from this that change was called for. 'This won't do,' she said sternly to herself and arranged with Deb to attend evening classes.

Lionel was at the class on Greek civilisation which had led, in time, to a study tour of the ancient sites of the Peloponnese. Emily had left her handbag in a restaurant, and Lionel had been gallant in retrieving it. After that, they had become a couple, of a kind. At weekends, Lionel visited Emily because her house was larger than his bachelor apartment. They walked, her arm in his, through the park and discussed Greek and other civilisations; and it was pleasant to have a body beside hers in bed at night, and a face to chat and read the papers with in the morning.

Lionel's introduction to Emily's children went better than she'd expected. 'He's nice, Mum,' Beth had said after a dinner where Emily had burned the leg of lamb in her anxiety over her daughters' pending judgement. 'You could do worse,' was Kate's more laconic view. The girls were glad their mother had someone to spend time with so that they needn't worry about her. So when Lionel asked Emily to marry him it seemed not a bad plan.

'Well, if you're sure,' Emily said. She didn't want another disappointment, not at her time of life.

'I wouldn't ask if I wasn't,' Lionel had said.

Perhaps there is some concealed trap-door which the vow to love and cherish unlatches but once they had signed their names in the local registry office, which was the last port of dreariness, the sense of companionship which had attracted Emily to Lionel began to slip away. Few people attended the ceremony – just the girls and Deb on Emily's side – Lionel had not asked anyone on his, which Emily vaguely noticed but at the time didn't trouble to ponder.

The honeymoon in Ravenna, where they admired the famous Byzantine mosaics, was only moderately passionate – but sensible people know not to expect too much of such occasions. Emily had learned her lesson with Mark. She kept her own counsel when Lionel complained about slow service in the laid-back local taverna and became irate over the matter of the lazy water pressure in their bathroom. And she did not take issue when he objected to the weather – unfortunately unseasonably inclement – though it was far from clear to her to whom his objections could usefully be addressed. But then, she thought, it is not every day, thank goodness, that one gets married and maybe it was his way of letting off steam.

It was Deb who said, 'Where have you gone? You know, I hardly see you these days.'

'I'm where I always was,' Emily retorted, sensing reproach. But was she? Deb's affection carried the pedigree of a tried-and-tested friendship and there was a hint of hurt in her tone which made Emily reflect. It was a long time since she and Deb had been out together. In the past, they had eaten regularly at each other's houses – or been to the pictures, or the theatre, or even taken odd weekends away. Now any meeting with Deb was mostly on the phone.

'I'm seeing Deb on Thursday.' As she spoke she experienced an emotion too fleeting to pin down but it was relief she felt when Lionel merely said, 'You've not seen her for a while, have you?' Deb had suggested they meet for a film but after it was over Emily hurried home and did not take up Deb's invitation to go back to hers for a drink.

That Christmas Kate said, 'Mum, why are you wearing that old apron? You always used to dress up for Christmas dinner.'

The Christmas was not proceeding well. Kate had invited a boyfriend, Robert, from Bristol. He smoked joints in the spare bedroom and, partly to steer the smoking outdoors, Emily offered the couple the loan of her car.

'It's my car,' Emily said protestingly when Lionel suggested that a boyfriend on drugs was 'too irresponsible' to be trusted. 'Anyway, cannabis is practically legal these days and it's no worse than you drinking gin and tonic.' She didn't add – too many gin and tonics! Perhaps it was politeness which made her refrain; or perhaps it was some other emotion. But whatever in the world was there to be afraid of? Lionel was 'nice' – hadn't Beth said so?

'Mum,' Beth said, washing up in the kitchen when Kate and Robert had gone for a spin in Emily's car. 'You've gone all quiet. What's happened? Cat got your tongue?'

Emily said she was feeling a bit whacked.

'You look it,' Beth said. 'Is everything OK? You're not ill, are you?'

Emily said she wasn't; but she found herself almost looking forward to her daughters' departure. It would be welcome to have the fine veil of anxiety, which seemed to have settled on her since their arrival, lifted. After Beth and Kate, and Robert, had been driven to the station Lionel said, 'I think we might go somewhere next year – get away from Christmas.'

'Oh why?' she blurted, at once regretting it.

'I hate Christmas,' Lionel said. 'All that fuss.'

Emily felt an upsurge of alarm. She had recognised there had been nothing even faintly seasonal about his attitude to the recent festivities, but the vehemence with which he was voicing dissatisfaction was disturbing.

'Oh, but I don't mind . . .'

'But I do. You might think of someone other than yourself for a change.'

Slicing onions at the time, she nearly sliced off the top of her thumb. At least the blood – crimson, like the brilliant berries on the holly branches which Kate had brought back from their drive in the country – was a distraction. Late that afternoon, Emily made a bonfire of all the Christmas paper debris and stood by the flames as the sky turned from pale to dark pewter and stray cawing birds came home to roost for the night.

The following year Kate rang and said, 'I hope you don't mind, Mum, but we won't be joining you for Christmas. Robert's mum has asked us . . .'

Emily said she didn't 'mind'. What else could she say? 'What about Beth?'

'Oh, Bethie's joining us too. It'll give you and Lionel a chance to be together without us getting in the way.'

'But, darling, you're *not*, you've never either of you been "in the way" . . .' Emily's heart, bunched hard, was hurting under her ribs.

'Yes, but Lionel . . . you know, Mum. It's better, really . . .'

'It looks as if it'll be just the two of us for Christmas. What would you like to do?' she said that evening.

'Nothing. Christmas is best avoided.' He didn't even call it 'humbug', a word which at least has a touch of life to it.

'We could always go to church.'

'Over my dead body!'

'You don't want me to make any preparations?'

'You please yourself. You always do.'

How has this happened? she asked herself, putting on her old coat to creep out to the park. It was as if she had been in an accident so serious she had not even noticed she was damaged until she tried to walk. Something drastic seemed to have occurred in the region of her spine. Returning home she rang Deb, but a message announced she would be away till the New Year. Once she and Deb had not gone out for an evening without informing each other of their respective movements.

I am alone, Emily said to herself, kneeling by the phone still in her coat. And I have done this to myself. The admission of responsibility made nothing better.

On Christmas morning, Emily woke before Lionel, whose body lay in the bed, well away from hers, his mouth a little open and a slight dribble of spittle visible on his chin. In the past, she might have felt tender at so naked a show of vulnerability. Now she didn't even feel disgust. Anxious not to wake him, she slid out of bed and went downstairs to the kitchen to make herself tea. Outside there was a thick rime on the lawn and she watched a coal tit peck ferociously at the bacon rind she had hung for the birds on the lilac tree. A white lilac, which she had bought when she and Lionel married. It had never bloomed.

A card – one of the few they had received that year – from Beth and Kate, of the magi, on camels, following the star, was propped on the table. I'll go to church, she thought. That at least will be some kind of celebration.

Having nothing better to do, Emily washed the kitchen floor before putting on boots and gloves for the walk to church. She thought of popping back upstairs to say where she was off to. Maybe better to leave a note which he could ignore if he chose. On the back of the envelope from Beth and Kate's card, she wrote, 'Gone to church'. Then, after a moment's reflection, she added, 'Join me, if you like'.

As is so often the case when one has all the time in the world, by the time Emily set out for the service she was pressed and had to hurry. The pews were already packed when she arrived. She squeezed her way past a row of unyielding knees to a seat near the back of the church and knelt and made a silent prayer: Please, let it come right in the end.

She was singing 'O Come All You Faithful' when

she saw Lionel. He had obviously arrived after her and was standing unobtrusively in one of the side aisles. Well, what a nice surprise – so prayers were sometimes answered. He had repented and come after her. They could walk home together, arm in arm, maybe through the park, and have a companionable Christmas after all.

After the service, Emily looked about for her husband but he must have slipped away. Maybe he hadn't wanted her to know he was in church. But at least he had joined her, which was a start.

Emily's heart was uncommonly buoyant as she walked back beneath the bright December sky. Never say die, she said to herself. Back home, she lit the oven for the farm chicken she had bought just in case. Looking out of the window, she saw that the tits had finished off the bacon rind and the lilac had blossomed, a delicate white, the colour of the frost. But that was strange. And when she went upstairs in search of Lionel, she found him where she had left him in bed that morning – stone cold, with the spittle on his chin quite dry.

EPIPHANY

The maroon-and-cream country bus, the only one that ran that day on account of it being the holiday season, was late and it was already dark when the young man reached the crossroads at the top of the hill. Before him, the lights of the town cascaded into the creased steel of the water below. Way out, at the farthest reach of his vision, a fishing boat was trawling the horizon, carrying with it a frail cargo of two beads of greenish light.

It was colder than he had bargained for and he missed a scarf as he walked downhill towards the sea. The road was as familiar to his feet as to his mind. Maybe more so; the body has its own memory.

He had walked there so often as a child, envisaging the world he was going to escape to, a world wide with promise, a match for his elastic imagination. 'Charlie,' his gran used to say, 'is made for better things than here.'

A cat slithered past his legs, a strip of skinny orange fur, and he wondered what 'better' meant to his gran. Fast cars and manicured blondes well turned out, in nightclubs, probably. Long ago, his gran had been a dancer herself, and in marrying a fisherman had come down in the world, in her own eyes.

He had been brought up, mostly, by his gran as he didn't have a father to speak of. And his mother had had to work. Then a time came, he couldn't be quite sure when, when Ivor, a furniture remover who drove a van, appeared on the scene. He came round for Sunday lunch, which they never usually had, and his mother had smacked his leg because he had revealed it was the first time he had eaten pork roast. She married Ivor in the end and he gave his stepson his name, McGowan, and a measure of grudging security. But Charlie always knew that his real father would have been different.

At the bottom of the hill, he turned right along the promenade, which ran alongside the unmindful water. Wrought-iron lampposts shed a lofty and undiscriminating light on a man peeing. The man shuffled round, setting his back towards Charlie, making a token gesture towards an embarrassment which neither of them felt.

Charlie continued along the promenade until it began to veer back towards the town and then ducked under the railings, and waded through inhospitable pebbles towards a hut, where, in the summer, ice cream and confectionery and hot dogs were sold. He leaned his back against the shuttered little structure and lit a cigarette, waiting.

He had smoked two cigarettes and was lighting a third before a car came to a stop in the road beside the hut. The car door banged to and then the heavy crunching tread of a dark shape of a man came towards him.

For a moment, Charlie thought the man was aiming a gun at him, then he realised it was a hand. He took the hand warily and shook it.

'Charles?'

'Charlie. Charles if you like.'

'Charlie then. I found you.'

'Yes.'

'Shall we walk, Charlie?'

They walked along the pebbled shore while the waves made audible little flirtatious sallies and withdrawals at their feet.

'You like the sea?' The voice was deep but awkwardness made it rise unnaturally.

'It's OK. You get tired of it, growing up beside it.'

'I never did.' There was a tint of reproach in the voice now.

'You live beside the sea, then?'

'I live by it. Your mum not tell you I was a fisherman?'

'She never told me anything about you.'

'Can't say I blame her. She was all right, your mum. A firebrand.' It wasn't easy, Charlie thought, talking to a man you'd never met whose face you couldn't even see. 'How did you find me then, if your mum told you nothing?'

'My gran kept an address.'

'Ah, she liked me, your gran. I sent you presents, birthday and Christmas.'

'When's my birthday, then?' Charlie said, hoping to catch him out.

'May twelfth, five fifteen in the morning, just in time to meet the morning catch.'

'I never got any presents.'

'I did wonder.'

Behind them, along the promenade, a car hooted and the harsh voices of some youths rang out, 'Fuck you!' 'Fuckin' madman! Fuck it!' 'Fuck off!'

'Language,' said the man walking beside Charlie. It was hard to tell whether the comment was a reproof or merely an observation.

'Mum never let me swear.'

It wasn't true. But he felt a weird obligation to assert a spurious vigilance on his mother's part, to distance her from this discovered act of treachery. For more years than he could bear to calculate, he

34

had longed for some token from his father. The news that this had been denied him, deliberately withheld, prompted a general defensiveness.

'She was all right, your mum.'

Charlie detected that this was the man's mantra against some cause for bitterness and tact made him draw back for a moment before lobbing the question: 'Why'd you leave her then?'

'That what she told you?'

In a moment of unspoken agreement, they had stopped and were looking out over the sea. The slate surface shimmered provocatively under the beam of the lamps on the long posts and the diffused lights of the windows of the bungalows, way up on Fulborough Heights.

'She say I left her, then?' the man asked again. There was an undertow of something in his voice Charlie recognised.

'Didn't you?' Any notion that there could be doubt over this was fantastic. He had been raised in the sure and certain knowledge that he had an absconding father. And yet there was that pleading animal tone.

'She chucked me out.'

'What for?' Relief that there might be another explanation for his father's dereliction struggled with the stronger fear that he was going to be asked to accommodate worse news.

'Didn't rate me, I guess.'

They had reached the farthest point of the beach's curve and, with the same accord with which they had stood surveying the dappled waves, the two men turned to walk back the way they had come. Charlie dug his hands in his pockets against the wind, conscious as he did so that he was adopting a pose he had absorbed from films. The gesture was a feeble understudy for the words needed to voice what he was feeling.

'Your dad was a right bastard,' he had heard his mother declare time and again. 'Walked out and left me with a bawling kid to cope with. Mind you,' she had added, when the black mood was on her, 'the way you go on, you'd have driven him out even if he hadn't gone before.'

'Your mum's mum, your gran, wanted me to stay,' the man who was his father resumed. 'Maybe I should've. I've often wondered what was right.'

'Yes,' Charlie said. 'Maybe you should.' As he said it he was aware of a dreadful gratitude emanating from the presence beside him. It seemed bizarre to make someone glad to learn that they had not done what you ardently wished they had done.

'You missed me, then?' The voice was now unquestionably wistful.

'Yeah, I missed you,' Charlie consented. He felt sick at his own words.

'Missed' wasn't the size of it. He had mourned

36

his absent father, fiercely, inconsolably, endlessly, desperately. Since he could remember thinking his own thoughts, missing his father had taken the lion's share of his inner life. It was, he suddenly recognised, to seek his father that he had made his way to London, for the only way to bear the loss had been to conjure that impossibly glamorous figure, whose flight it was possible to condone on grounds of innate superiority. He could never have envisaged this hesitant man with the unsettling squeak and tremor in his voice. Sharply, fervently, he wished this newly recovered parent to the bottom of the sea.

'And you are a fisherman?' he said aloud in response to a solicitude he had come, over the years, to resent but had never had the heart to forswear.

'Was is the operative word. I don't do anything now. No work for us fisher folk these days, what with the EEC.'

The note of whimsy was terrible. An unemployed, down-at-heel, shabby fisherman was no substitute for an insouciant profligate high-hearted deserter. Charlie, acute to personal danger, braced himself for further unwanted revelation.

'I live with a decent woman. Pat. She sees me right. Works up at the local pub and helps out with the B and B there. I do odd jobs for them too. We get by. What do you do?'

'I'm an actor.' Pause. 'Well, trying to be. But . . .'

'It's hard, I know. You've got the voice.'

'Have I?' Charlie felt a shot of excitement at this unexpected encouragement.

'A good voice, you've got. I heard it straight away. I had a voice once. Someone put me in a film. Said I was a natural. Offered to take me to Hollywood.'

'Really?' Suspicion of this hint of redeeming enterprise in his lost parent hovered over relief.

'I'm not a liar,' Charlie's father said placidly. They had reached the beach hut again and he stopped and took out a packet of cigarettes. 'Untipped, they are. Got the habit on the boats.'

'Hard to get, aren't they now?'

'I'm not a liar,' his father repeated, cradling the match with which he lit Charlie's cigarette with a big hand. Red lobster hands. 'I didn't leave your mum. She didn't want me. Don't blame her. But I shouldn't have left you.'

Charlie stood, looking out at the glimmer of the receding tide, pulling on his father's cigarette. A strand of tobacco had stuck to his lip. The words he had longed to hear, had rehearsed to himself so often, in bed at night, crying himself to sleep after his mother had been having a go, 'I shouldn't have left you', bounced away into the unpitying darkness. He felt nothing. Not even contempt. It was a poor sort of an offering from a prodigal father.

'I'm glad you've come to see her, anyway,' he said at last.

'I'd've come sooner if you'd asked.'

'Yes,' Charlie said. 'I know. I should have asked you before.' It was a kind of acknowledgement between the two of them.

'Better late than never,' said his father. Through the darkness Charlie could just make out that he was grinning. 'Shall we go in my car?'

'I don't have one. I came by bus.'

Walking through the hospital corridors, which smelled of nothing normal, Charlie looked at his father for the first time. Broad shoulders, middle height, hair once dark, now mostly grey, a face which might have been handsome once but had settled into hangdog, jeans, donkey jacket, with a sprinkling of dandruff about the shoulders, visible white vest, plaid wool shirt, brown suede shoes, wrong shade for the rest of what he was wearing. A model of unexceptional ordinariness. Except that he was the father he had never had – and at the same time he was not. He was quite another father. A stranger.

'I bought her a present,' Charlie's new father said, producing a box from his pocket. 'Roses choco-lates. Too late for Christmas, but she used to like Roses. Mind you, she liked hard centres best, Jen, but I thought in the circumstances soft centres might go down better.'

Charlie did not say that his mother was past eating anything, even soft centres. Nor did he consciously form the thought, but in the region of his mind, which as yet had formed no words, he became aware that he was in charge of these two beings, his parents. An access of violent tenderness waylaid him and he touched his father's arm. 'She'll be glad you remembered.'

'Think so?' The blue eyes were horribly beseeching. A hurt child's eyes. 'Bit late for Christmas but . . .'

'I'm sure so,' Charlie said, untruthfully. He was not at all sure how his mother would take this. It had been an impulse to follow up the address he had found in his gran's oak bureau when he cleared it after she died. It was written on a corner of torn-off card, which, from the faint trace of glitter, and the suggestion of a robin's breast, looked as if it had been sent one Christmas. He had guessed at once whom the card had come from.

They were approaching his mother's ward, which, in deference to her condition, was shared by only two other patients. 'Both on their way out' as his stepfather had observed. Ivor, Charlie guessed, was counting his wife's definitely numbered days to the time he could settle down to widowerhood and a story of suffering nobly borne.

Charlie's mother's was the first bed in the ward

and, as was customary now, she was behind drawn curtains, as if she was rehearsing what it would be like to have the curtains drawn for good.

'Mum?'

'What? Oh, it's you. You're back, then.'

'Mum, I've brought a visitor.'

Across the face, once pretty, now bleached by years of discontent and disappointment, and further diminished by drugs and pain, flashed a sudden enlivening angry interest. 'Who is it?'

Charlie's father stepped forward, jolting the bedside cupboard so that the jug of water on it rocked perilously. 'It's me, Jen.'

'Mind that jug. Who's "me", when you're at home?'

But she knew. And Charlie knew that she knew. And in that instant he knew that he had done something remarkable. Unquestionably, unmistakably, his mother was pleased. Relief rushed in on him, warming him like a double Scotch on an empty stomach.

'It's Jeff, Jen.'

'My God!'

'No, your Jeff!' For a moment, there was something that Charlie saw in his father's face. Charm.

'I don't believe it!'

'All right if I sit down, Jen?'

'Sit here.' Charlie's father sat on the bed where she had gestured and Charlie saw that his mother's face had grown not pale but pink. 'I don't believe it,' she said again. 'How did you get here?'

'Him.' Charlie's father nodded towards their son. 'He found me. Wrote to me. Said you were ill and . . .'

'I'm dying, you know that, don't you?'

Charlie, who had had strict instructions from his stepfather to keep this news from his mother, felt a further rush of absolving relief.

'It's why I came, Jen.'

'He tell you that?' Charlie's mother gestured towards him.

'No. I guessed. You don't mind me coming?'

''Course I don't, you daft 'appeth.'

Charlie said, 'I'm going for a smoke and a wander. I'll be back in a bit.'

He walked down the corridor, where he met the duty sister. 'Mum's got another visitor,' he explained. He didn't want anyone spoiling anything by blundering in with a change of her bag, or whatever.

'That's nice. Who is it?'

'A relative. They've not seen each other in a while.'

'Ah, nice,' the sister said, vaguely benign. 'It's one of the good things about the Christmas season. People get together again who mightn't otherwise.'

She had a point, Charlie granted, staring at the hospital Christmas tree. It was still decked, though it was twelfth night, still bearing brightly wrapped faux presents. His gran would have said it was the Devil's luck not to have that all down by now. Or was it the last day they could safely be up before the bad fairies dropped out of the greenery to work their harm? What was it happened today? He'd forgotten. His gran would surely have told him.

He went outside for a smoke and looked at the saucepan in the night sky. We Three Kings of Orientar, he remembered suddenly. On their camels following the star. Bringing gifts, gold, frankincense and . . . he couldn't remember the last one.

When he returned to the ward, his father was still sitting on the bed holding his sleeping mother's hand. She looked peaceful. Myrrh, he suddenly remembered. That was the other one. Myrrh. They put it on dead bodies, his teacher had told them at school. Death had its good side. Because his mother was dying, he'd found his father. But when she was dead and gone he would have to live with the find. Be careful what you look for, you might find it, his gran had sometimes said.

The box of Roses chocolates, like a small wayside altar, stood unopened beside the jug of water on the bedside cupboard.

Noting Charlie's glance, his father said, 'She says she'll have one later.'

'D'you want to go?'

'Better had. Pat'll be . . . But I'll come again, if . . .?'

'Yeah, sure.'

'I'll bring Pat. That's if . . .'

'Yeah, sure.'

'Perhaps I won't. She didn't mind, did she, Jen, that I came?'

A lifetime of minding. Minding for her as well as for himself. Minding her taunts, her viciousness. Minding her accusations. Minding her furious campaigns against his life, and, almost worse – for there was no way he could help or stop her – her own. Excusing her fits of temper, her cruelty, her unpredictable hysteria because she had suffered this shocking injustice. Was it simply that she'd made a mistake? Sent away a man who loved her and then regretted it? Could she so not acknowledge the enormity of what she had done that she had hidden behind this bogus story, this piece of twisted, pointless, self-justifying confabulation? Or was she just an out and out liar? How could he tell now? He'd had to make a life without his father, and soon he would be making it without his mother. And who were they anyway, his father and his mother? How would he ever know now?

'She was pleased with the chocolates, wasn't she?' his father said. 'She loved chocolates, Jen did. I used to buy them for her: Roses, Quality Street. It wasn't true, you know, about them asking me to Hollywood. I wanted them to. I'd have gone. But

I reckon the film wasn't any great shakes after all. And they didn't ask.'

'Yes,' Charlie said. He looked at his father's red lobster hands, clenching and unclenching. 'I expect she was pleased about the chocolates.'

'Yes,' said his father. 'She did seem pleased, didn't she?'

THE DRAGON'S BONES

(for Penelope Fitzgerald)

her head lay against his shoulder through the anxious nights.

The truth was, the *pensione* was more than he could easily reach to, but to tell her was one of the many things he could not afford. The cost of the tiny cups of coffee and trays of daintily dressed snacks and drinks, which she ordered with charming ease, accumulated at the back of his thoughts, like dust in an over-used vacuum-cleaner bag, waiting to burst and pollute the pure sea air which smacked their faces heartily each morning.

To be fair, she was not aware that he was stretched. It was innocently that she executed her costly little commands. 'Shall we have a drink?' Or 'I'm starving, let's send down for one of their cheese-and-ham thingies, shall we?' The steady traffic of hotel platters filled him with a terrified unease: he was far from certain that the credit on his card was going to meet the bill at the end of their stay.

And it had been his idea to come – he who had carried her off here with such promise and aplomb; she had not angled for it – there was no question of her throwing herself at his head; so that he could not now say, 'Go easy' or even suggest a picnic in the Giardini Pubblici, where they had passed old men muffled up in scarves, and whores in leather coats relaxing in the brilliant winter sun. One of the whores had caught his eye and he had been worried that the girl had noticed. It was lucky, he reflected – feeling guilty at the thought – that she watched her weight, for otherwise she might have demanded some grand repast as recompense. His happiness in her company was daily compromised by the fear that she might suddenly suggest dinner at one of those frighteningly grand hotels – the Danieli or, please God not, the Cipriani.

So that when, lying on her stomach on the bed, her legs crossed and swinging back and forth over her bottom like a much younger girl – his kid sister, for example, as he remembered her before their mother died – she had found, in the pages of the guidebook, a reference to some bones in the old church of Murano, the island where they blew glass, it was the greatest relief to him. Here was an opportunity for benevolence which could cost no more than a boat-ride. And he so longed to indulge her.

'A princess should see a dragon, of course!' He was a little in love with his own humorous riposte.

The refracted light from the water, as they waited for the vaporetto, settled on her like a blessing or a prayer. She stood, perched on her high-heeled boots, like some exotic teetering crane bird. The big coat she was wrapped in contributed to the sense of feathers. She had been wearing it, the pale grey coat, that day he had seen her first – in the park, sitting on a bench reading, where he had stopped to sit too, drawn by her grave absorption in what she read. There had been a stillness about her, he remembered now.

He compressed his eyes against the sun to observe her better. She was watching for the boat. There was something childlike about her imperious wish that each of the craft which called at the landing-stage be theirs; so that when at last theirs did arrive, he felt sufficiently free of the constraining worry to be able to tease her just a little, once they had found their way aboard, and to tuck safe in under her hat a fair strand of hair which the salt wind was whipping about. It was good to take charge.

They sat at the nose of the boat where the wind flirtatiously competed with her over the hat.

'Take it off,' he suggested; and she did, so that later, she remarked, stepping out on to the landing-stage at Murano, that the wind must have left her looking 'like a witch' and, clearly, that must have been his intention – so that no one else would look at her but him.

He had to fight off a certain surliness descending at this, for somewhere in his mind there was, indeed, the thought that he wanted her to himself; wanted to be rid of the calculating glances of men who appraised her young body. His own body was far from young.

Passing a trattoria on the fondamenta, where a waiter was already laying out the tables – securing paper cloths at the corners with steel clips against the wind – he imagined, as he steered her through the narrow gap, the waiter's cynical black eyes following them and determined they would not go back there for lunch.

The church was old, twelfth century the guide-book said. It quoted Ruskin and he took a certain pride in knowing who Ruskin was and why his opinion was worth hearing. 'Ruskin praised it,' he explained to her, 'but then it was restored later on in the nineteenth century,' and she gave a slight shudder as if to reassure him that she knew that such barbarous practices were to be deplored.

But restoration or no they agreed it was unde-niably beautiful – the old mellow brick church.

Inside, they stood, slightly awed, together on the threshold of the ancient billowing floor. Before them, in the dim curve of the apse above the altar, there hovered an elongated figure.

Set in an unadorned vista of scintillating gold, the young mother of God held up her palms in an attitude of naked supplication, as if, surprised by some interloper, she were protecting her modesty. Instinctively, he crossed himself, and genuflected, making the gesture of obeisance.

'You're not Catholic!' she exclaimed.

He had never said – why should he? He no longer practised; but there was something exasperating in the way she had spoken.

He felt intruded upon, and bundled away the feeling with an attempt at casualness. 'Not now. But it sort of sticks.'

His wife's face, puckered in angry astonishment the day he had told her he was leaving, interposed itself between the vision of the blue-gowned Virgin in her gold-tasselled stole.

'Oh no,' she said, 'I like it that you are,' and he felt annoyed with himself for feeling grateful. The marriage vows were for life – his wife had sent fat, voluble Father Michael to remind him.

'It is a mortal sin you are committing, Joseph, to leave your lawful married wife, now. One that the Holy Father in His blessedness, mind, can never forgive.'

A bleak ember of anger began to smoulder again, threatening to break into that consuming flame. She came across and put her arm in his. 'You can show me, then,' she suggested, 'all the churchy bits I don't understand.'

But most of the church was a puzzle to him too, hardly like the churches he knew from home at all. Those were modern, with coloured paper flowers on the altar, and new pine, waxy and yellow. This one seemed a kind of emporium of pagan imports – on the worn marble floor peacocks picked at grain, a fox was unfathomably strung between two roosters; and the leaf-scrolled capitals crowning the grey-granite columns seemed to belong more in a pagan temple than a church. Only the slight young woman, in the background of soaring gold, with the still more golden halo round her chaste head, was familiar to him.

'I expect they took half this stuff over from earlier times,' she said, comfortingly. 'Anyway, it's all worship, isn't it?'

They stood before a bank of glimmering candles, the long youthful Virgin above them. From the guidebook he read aloud, *'The relics of St Donato are in the church; also, the relics of the dragon he killed may be seen behind the high altar.'*

'There!' she pointed. Four lanky ribs hung incongruously suspended beneath the Virgin, who rested lightly, on one foot, on her cushion above. 'See, the dragon!'

'It must be a bull or an ox or something, I suppose,' he mused.

'No, it's a dragon. It says so.' She was prettily defiant.

'Yes,' he said, prepared to be amused, 'of *course* it is a dragon.'

'You don't believe it?'

'Well . . .' he was at a loss, not knowing what she wanted. He had tried to play the game: 'Not really, but . . .'

'But you believe in the Holy Ghost – Spirit – whatever you call it. Why not dragons?'

He didn't know that he did believe in the Holy Spirit: fat Father Michael had spoken of eternal damnation. 'It is hell now you are looking to spend your unnatural days in, Joseph.'

'Dragons are legend.' His voice in the huge church sounded squeaky and insignificant. To his alarm he heard a crack in it – it would be terrible if he were to cry in front of her. 'The Holy Spirit's different.' He pressed his voice into a cheerful certainty he was hardly equal to feeling.

'Why? Why is it different?' She was frowning now. A group of people had come into the church. A guide, a woman, was pointing with an unfurled umbrella at the all-comprehending Virgin. 'Isn't your religion all legend too? You believe that *she*,' her rising voice made the underlining, 'was fucked by God, don't you?'

The candid eyes of the blue-robed Virgin, whose hands seemed so uncompromisingly to ward off evil, gazed down upon them. He had lied to his wife – pretended that there was no one he was leaving for. 'We were married too young, Josie,' he had said, trying desperately to staunch her weeping furious questions. Had it made any difference that they had, both of them, almost the same name? Maybe it prevented him from seeing Josie as she was – different from him. But that wasn't true either. Once, if you had asked him, he would have said he would have died for his young bride. People where he came from didn't ask such things – but there was no one he would have died for since as he would have done for Josie.

'Yes, but . . .' The truth was he was shocked. How did you explain the Immaculate Conception?

'I don't rubbish your beliefs – you shouldn't mine.'

It was the picture of her, in her grey fluffy coat bent over her book, for which he had left Josie; his daughter now would not even let him visit his grandchildren. He felt the back of his throat prick again. 'I wasn't rubbishing . . .' He knew she knew that he wasn't. This was one of those inexplicable, unpredictable things which women did to you – pretended you were treating them badly when all the time they must know how hard you were trying. He had been so pleased to take her to see the dragon's bones. And Josie – there was no help for it. In his heart he knew he had treated her badly.

The girl turned away and stalked down the side aisle towards the door. She no longer looked like a bird – unless it were something wild and dangerous which might flash suddenly at you with its beak and cut your flesh to the bone. To his horror he saw she was about to address the guide of the party. In this mood she might say anything.

Hurrying after her he understood suddenly, why, in the days before he left, Josie had gone about the house without a bra. Her nipples protruding through her cardigan had startled, then revolted him. He had backed away from the thought of it. Now, in a flash, he saw that she had been trying – poor Josie – to rekindle his interest in her.

He caught up with the girl and grabbed her arm just as he heard her say, 'Excuse me, the dragon . . .?'

'*Si, signora*?' The guide, a short stocky woman with a white face and a faint trace of moustache, stared at them with a tincture of insolence. It must have been obvious they were having a row.

'We were wondering – St Donato killed it . . . when?'

'It was eight, nine century, *signora*.'

'And was it why he was made a saint?'

Looking down at the intricate marble patterns of the floor he was conscious of the Virgin's measureless blue gaze above.

'*Si, signora*. He kill the dragon which make all the people afraid.'

'You see,' she said, triumphant, disengaging his grip from her arm and placing her own under his, 'even your stupid old Church believed in it!'

She was smiling again, and in a rush of joy that the matter of the dragon had been settled – slaughtered for good, he hoped – and that she was back with him again, he was about to propose lunch in the trattoria they had passed when she continued:

'Where shall we go for lunch?' – and before he could answer – 'Or, let's just have a snack now, shall we? Then we can eat properly for once tonight. At the Danieli, or that one I read about, where the film-stars go, the Cipriani. We can, now, can't we . . .?'

THE HAWTHORN MADONNA

Every Easter, Elspeth and Ewan stayed in a cottage loaned them by Mrs Stroud, who had been a school friend of Ewan's Aunt Val. Not that the two old ladies ever saw much of each other in their latter days. Still, it was recognisably Edie Stroud in Aunt Val's photo album – the girl with the almost coal-black hair, very bobbed – unless that was Mary Squires, after all, who died of tuberculosis after her fiancé shot himself. When Mrs Stroud herself died, the cottage passed to her nephew who worked in Amsterdam – something to do with diamonds, someone had said, though that might have been wishful thinking. He was glad enough to let it without trouble to a couple who did not mind that there was a greenish fungus around the window frames and that you had to hang the bedding before the fire to air each night before you went to sleep. Indeed, they would have missed the nightly ritual, Elspeth and Ewan, if Mrs Stroud's nephew had done what his aunt had always been saying she would do and have a proper damp course laid down.

Luckily, Mrs Stroud herself was now laid down instead and the fingers of moisture were allowed to settle inside the glass of the windows unhindered and make little feathery rivulets down the pane and emanate out into the general air of the place.

Elspeth and Ewan had never had any children. In the early days when they went to 'Brow' they had gone with the plan of serious lovemaking. But as anyone who has ever tried it knows 'serious' lovemaking is not the most successful kind. When it became clear that for one reason or another (they never tried too hard to discover which) they were not going to have children they tacitly dropped such plans. This did not mean that they were not affectionate with each other. People often said of them that they were an exceptionally warm couple – really, it did you good to be with them. In bed at night they held each other close even years after the lovemaking had been dropped altogether, except for birthdays and Christmas. But it was Easter when they always went to 'Brow' which seemed not quite to qualify . . .

This Easter was particularly cold, though Elspeth said that all Easters were cold these days and it must be to do with climate change. She believed that something had happened to the calendar since they were young. Not at all, Ewan said. The Met Office had produced statistics which demonstrated that the weather had been much the same, give or take the odd fluctuation, for the past two hundred years. That was just like men, Elspeth had retorted, to dismiss everything the scientists tell us if it didn't suit their prejudices. They were driving, as usual, down the M3 and off the A303 past Stonehenge and into the heart of Somerset, if such a promiscuous county could be said to have a 'heart'.

The cottage was called 'Brow' because it stood on the brow of a low hill – hardly a hill at all, really, more a kind of hump. It stood alone at the end of a lane, which fortunately had never been surfaced and therefore discouraged picnickers.

Elspeth unpacked the box of groceries she had brought from London to save having to go too often to Brack, the nearest village, or to Wells for decent wine. Ewan went at once to inspect the woodshed. Yes, plenty of sawn logs stacked – so Tim, the young man who seemed always to be smoking joints but who for all that kept the hedges neatly clipped, had done his stuff. And there were enough candles too for when the electricity tripped off. All in order, then. And it never took long to heat up the tank for a bath.

It was still cold the next day when they went for

one of the walks which over the years they had taken possession of – behind the hill and along the track through the plantation, towards Wells. You could just see the twin honey-coloured cathedral towers in the distance below them. 'Shall we go to Wells tomorrow?' Elspeth asked. 'Tomorrow' was Good Friday. But in the end they decided not – it wasn't a big thing with them, church at Easter – just that Elspeth liked the pageantry.

'It's going to snow,' Ewan remarked as he opened the wine for supper. They were to have *boeuf en daube*, brought all the way from Highgate in a casserole. Years ago Elspeth had learned the recipe from reading *To the Lighthouse* but these days she never imagined herself as Mrs Ramsey.

'"Nudity banned until this appears in hedges" – eight letters?' Ewan asked later by the fire. Although Elspeth had quite a different cast of mind, and never got crossword clues, for twenty years he had persevered in asking her advice.

'Hawthorn,' she said, proving that it is right never to stop trying.

'Why so?'

'"Ne'er cast a clout till may be out." People think it's the month, but in fact it's the may flower. Don't you remember? I've told you that millions of times!' But a mind that grasps crosswords will usually be too reasonable for rhymes or folklore.

Perhaps it was the extreme temperature but by

Saturday Ewan had contracted a cold. They ate toasted hot-cross buns by the fire and he went to bed early. Elspeth wished they had packed whisky and Ewan wished she wouldn't fuss.

'It's not "fussing" to want you to have a good time!'

'I'll be right as rain tomorrow,' Ewan said.

But he wasn't. Elspeth was aware that his night had been restless. Years of sleeping alongside her husband's tall frame had attuned her own to his. When he slept badly so did she – one of the penalties of a successful partnership. By morning he was coughing alarmingly and even – more alarming – agreed to stay in bed.

There is only so much attention you can give a reluctant invalid. By afternoon Ewan shooed Elspeth out for a walk. 'But where shall I go? I don't want to do one of ours without you.' Ewan thought this daft but Elspeth, who could be stubborn, had her own rules. Well, she would strike out, find somewhere new, then when he was better they could explore it together, add it to the others they had made their own over the years.

Although the walks Elspeth liked best started from the cottage door, there was no chance she could discover new territory that way – it was all too well tried. So it would have to be a car trip, which would give her a chance to buy whisky – she felt that the least she could do for Ewan was provide that. Wells had a Majestic. She would go that way and then on towards Glastonbury, never mind the old hippies.

With a bottle of Glenfiddich in the back of the car, Elspeth felt more entitled to her outing. But even then she wasn't about to abandon her husband altogether. She would keep him with her by doing what she and Ewan had done when they had first met – drive where fancy took you, then take every left turn until you found the place you were looking for; it always worked in the end.

Elspeth drove by instinct, following roads she had never travelled until all she knew was that she had come some way from Wells. But wasn't Somerset a strange county? Even such a short distance from where she had started the snow was quite deep, lining the hedges with precarious spines of powdery white. The white gave her a chill feeling. She half wished she had packed a thermos flask. There, she hoped she was not becoming one of those people who forever wished they had done things differently! She had the whisky, after all. Left, left, left again – it was funny, when you thought about it, that you so rarely came back on yourself – left here, and here and here – now stop.

She had fetched up in a dead-end – not so much a dead-end because there remained ahead a track which a lighter vehicle could traverse but not the Volvo. Plenty of room for a person though.

Elspeth stepped out of the car pulling on her fleece-lined anorak. Would she take the whisky just for the fun of a nip? No, it was for Ewan; unsealed it was not so much of a present. Lucky she had brought her boots.

The snow was melting into the mud as Elspeth walked along the lane. On either side the hedges grew high, covered in wild clematis and the fine, light dusting of particles of snow which gave the wrong seasonal feel: it was Easter not Christmas. Although still early afternoon the light had begun to fail – or perhaps more snow was gathering, blocking out the weak sun. Now there was a wooden gate ahead, its mossy slats slightly out of true – and just beyond Elspeth made out a small stone building with a cross aloft. A chapel.

Despite her expectations, the door of the chapel yielded quite naturally and Elspeth stepped inside. A sweetish, musky smell greeted her – not altogether disagreeable, but not wholly pleasant either.

'You can put the lights on if you like.'

The voice, neither low nor loud, was pitched from somewhere in the shadowy back part of the chapel – what in a church is called the apse.

'I'm sorry?' She wasn't alarmed yet.

'No need to be! The switch is on your left, just shoulder height.'

The chapel lit up to reveal a man seated on a bench at the wall farthest from the altar, on which were arranged thorny branches of green and flowering white. To the left there stood a slight wooden statue.

'See there, the Hawthorn Madonna,' said the man. 'We're proud of her here.' Although, since he was sitting down, it was hard to be sure, he appeared of medium height – quite ordinary, in fact.

'It looks old,' said Elspeth, trying to be polite.

But at this the man merely laughed – a brusque barking sound, like some large, indifferent seabird. 'You can touch her if you like.'

'Surely not!' A touch of reproof – Elspeth was only mildly religious but she knew what was to be respected.

'Why not? You won't hurt her. 'Sides, she's meant to be touched at Eastertide.'

Some local rite or ritual, Elspeth thought.

She walked forward, setting her boots down carefully on the flags. The figure was made of a knotty dark wood, with a natural-looking twist in it which greatly added to the feeling of something limber and flowing.

'Does she have a baby?' Elspeth did not know why she had asked this – nor even that she was going to ask it until the words flew, with a life of their own, from her lips. Once out, they seemed to hang in the air, with the breath which was making icy clouds before her face.

'Is it a baby you want, then?'

'Oh, yes!'

Once more, the words were out before she knew it but she had no thoughts of taking them back. After all, it was what had lain behind all her other thoughts, during the nights when she didn't sleep; maybe even more the ones she did.

'Touch her then and ask.'

It was odd how she didn't mind that he mentioned it – the subject she and Ewan had put away for good between them. But Ewan was at home, sick, and here she was in an unknown place – with a stranger . . .

Ewan said later that it was the whisky that had done it. 'She got me into bed, got me tight and raped me!' he used to say, and Elspeth would blush a little, perhaps because she didn't like the word 'rape' to be used of anything to do with Jack. On the other hand, she didn't want to take from Ewan his pride in their son – or her husband's part in creating him.

Jack was born, slightly premature, late on Christmas Day. But of course, Easter was early that year – and the may flowers were not out for a good few weeks after.

APHRODITE'S HAT

'Why is she wearing a hat?' I asked.

We were in the National Gallery at the time and looking at a painting by Cranach the Elder of Aphrodite and her son, Eros. He has been stung by a bee and they both are stark naked except that the Goddess of Love seems to be sporting a splendid hat, broad and flat and trimmed with feathers and set slantwise on her coquettish head. I could tell James was thinking about something else and didn't take in my question. It was rhetorical anyway; posed for myself, for some future enquiry.

James and I met occasionally at the National Gallery. It was close to where we both worked and we had long ago decided that it was safe to be together in a public place. We both had spouses, neither of whom worked in town. And there was no one likely to meet us there who knew us, though you can never tell. But these days it is not, in any case, uncommon for a man and a woman, who are friends, to meet in a lunch break. Nevertheless, there are pitfalls in conducting a love affair, even one as well organised as ours.

James and I had first met years ago at university. We had gone out together and then 'slept' together (which is what we called it then) in a rather fumbling incompetent way, with not much actual sleep but not unpleasant either. Then, for reasons neither of us could remember, we drifted apart.

There are few things more mysterious than endings. I mean, for example, when did the Greek gods end, exactly? Was there a day when Zeus waved magisterially down from Olympus and Aphrodite and her lover Ares, and her crippled husband Hephaestus (I always felt sorry for him), and all the rest got rolled up like a worn-out carpet? But with me and James it turned out not to have been an 'end' after all.

After we both left university, I married Pete, a research chemist, and James married Diane, who became a solicitor. It was pure chance (though is chance ever quite 'pure', I wonder?) that we all met years later at a party, quite an ordinary affair. It was James and I who encountered each other first and I remember he said, 'Oh, it's you, you never collected your sponge bag . . .' and I blushed, because I do blush, and because it's unnerving meeting someone you've been to bed with but haven't seen for over twenty years.

Later we discovered that neither of us had told our spouse about the other, which somehow made things easier. Not that we sprang into bed together again all at once.

It was James's son, Alastair, who prompted the revival. He was going for a university interview at Bristol and there was a train strike, so Diane said he could use the family car. James is an architect and had a house to see that day down in Sussex. Pete and I happened to be dining with them when all of this was being discussed and I could see a row was brewing over the dispensation of cars so I offered James a lift. I had to go to Brighton anyway and his appointment wasn't far out of my way. Sometimes I wonder if Diane would have been so pleased with this solution if she had known about me and James in the past.

My own appointment didn't take long. I'm a casting director and I had to see a new young possible for a projected screen test, a problematic, but definitely screen-desirable, boy of nineteen, and James's clients had decided to have a family rather than a refurbished house, so we ended up having lunch together, which went on rather longer than we both intended. And then at the end of it there still seemed more to say. Slightly awkwardly, we arranged another lunch and found we didn't want to stop. Funny, how much more passionate it was than at nineteen.

I looked again at the painting. It would have been fun casting Aphrodite. Her long, tilted, small-breasted body was undeniably erotic, and that hat on top of all that blatant nakedness . . .

We moved on to look at the Uccello of St George killing the dragon. I like this painting because it looks as if the princess has the dragon on a lead rather than her being held captive by him. 'Poor dragon,' I said, as I tended to. I've always been on the side of the beast in fairy stories.

James didn't say anything but he was never a great talker. I was the one who rattled on, and he liked me to do so because it allowed him space to think. His wife, Diane, tended to question him rather too much. So when he told me there was something he wanted to say, I guessed that all wasn't well.

We walked, as we did on such occasions, to the Italian restaurant where they suppose we are married. Or, they pretend they suppose. I don't know how many married couples in their late forties still hold hands. But these are Italians, and I cling to a sentimental notion that the Italians still look at things differently when it comes to matters of the heart.

'It's Diane,' James said, once he'd ordered the wine. 'She's not well.'

I've noticed that I only have to be working on a film for it to begin to resemble my own life. Or, more scarily, for my life to begin to resemble it. The film I was casting just then was called *Misdemeanour* and was about a middle-aged couple who have been childhood sweethearts and meet after twenty years and fall in love again. But the husband (at the time it was the husband but the director was toying with the idea of making it the wife instead – anyway, one of the lovers' partners) gets MS. It's a kind of ghastly pun, you see, MS demeanour = what is the correct 'demeanour' with which to meet multiple sclerosis? From which you will understand this is a supposedly arty film: one with a moral to it.

'Yes?' I said, carefully. It was implicit between us that we never put pressure on each other. Instinctively, I drew back.

'She may have, well, almost certainly has got, cancer.'

'Oh hell,' I said.

I could just as well have said nothing. 'You could always try saying nothing,' my husband, Pete sometimes remarks, when at times I have, untruthfully, suggested that I do not know what to say. I like Diane, you see. That's the hell of it. In another life she and I might have been friends, though not close friends. We aren't enough alike.

The wine arrived just then so we had the usual

courtesies of drawing the cork, which meant the conversation, too, was drawn, to a temporary pause. When James had tasted the wine and pronounced it 'fine', I asked, 'What kind?'

'Bladder,' said James briefly. I had guessed it might be breast, which of all the cancers, I have been given to understand, is the least bad. Diane had good breasts; mine were meagre affairs by comparison.

'Shit!' I allowed myself to say this time.

The starter arrived now, seafood salad for me and a pasta for James. Again we expressed fake enthusiasm and began to eat in silence. A silence that I broke: that was my role.

'I suppose it makes you feel badly about me,' I suggested. I didn't say 'us'. Even with James, 'us' is a term I fight shy of.

He didn't have to reply; I knew him so well. Sometimes I wondered why we even bothered to speak, except that I like to talk and he liked to hear me.

But more than that, I wondered why it took us so long to discover we loved each other? Why did we not recognise this all those years ago, as students back in Newcastle, when there was no one to hurt or be hurt by this sense of the two of us being joined, irrevocably and eternally, in some inexplicable linking light? Why had we so botched it then? Failed to perceive the potential for delight in the other's bone and skin, in misdeeds divulged, in shared observations – starlings scattering across a green dawn London sky, the subtle discretion of a wrinkle in a Rembrandt portrait, the plangent note of a Schubert song, the correct use of an unusual word or phrase – in the lovely, inimitable – and, oh why is this the test of tests? – *smell* of the beloved? Why, oh why, had we parted at nineteen and twenty only to come together at forty-five and forty-six? And why Pete and Diane, two utterly decent people, whom we both loved in another way? Why not a shrew and a monster? A harpy and a bully? Why not two utter beasts whom we could ethically and happily rid ourselves of . . . but 'beasts' would have been no help either – I liked beasts . . .

I recalled suddenly Uccello's dragon and then Aphrodite in her hat. It's *her* doing, I savagely thought. She, *she* has wantonly arranged this terrible timing.

James had finished his pasta, which he had eaten with ferocious rapidity, and was now breaking bread sticks into shards.

'I don't know what to do,' he said.

This was why I loved James. No, what am I saying? There was no 'why' about my loving James. I loved him from top to toe and inside out and back to front and reasons were superfluous. I wasn't besotted. I was aware that like everyone else he had his annoying side. It just didn't annoy me. There is no rhyme or reason to these things. But implicated in that love was the recognition that he wouldn't lie to me. And that meant he would never say what he didn't know he truly felt.

'I shouldn't think you do,' I said bleakly.

He has never said so, but with the part of me that 'knows' things in my bones I knew that if James loved me too it had to do with the fact that I never pushed him to feel things he didn't feel. Or, more important, not to feel things he did feel. Letting each other be as we were, and not as we might wish that we were, was one of the ways we matched.

Another was my habit of voicing seeming irrelevancies which weren't, so that what I said next had a connection.

'Perhaps that's why she kept her hat on,' I said, and it drifted into my mind that my godmother used to say 'Keep your hat on!' when anyone got agitated.

Another 'reason' for loving James was that he was quick. He didn't say much but his understanding was as swift as mine, so he didn't now say, as most men would, 'Who?' or 'Whose hat?' Although he had made no comment on the painting we had looked at that morning together he knew at once who I meant.

'Perhaps it's too dangerous if she's completely naked,' he agreed.

After that we were both silent again. Toni was

filleting my sole and making a fuss over whether we wanted spinach or carrots. I found that, quite desperately, I wanted spinach; you'd think, in the circumstances, I wouldn't give a damn. But when larger matters are beyond your control small things take on an especially vivid importance.

And, in case you are wondering, yes, of course I was thinking: Perhaps Diane will die and then James and I can go off together. But even in the fraction of a second it took to have that thought I knew that such an outcome would be hopeless. There was Pete, solid and kind and, so far as I knew, faithful – and there was Diane; dead or alive, she would matter. That was the point. She mattered to James and so she mattered to me. She was partly why he loved me, because I understood why she mattered.

I can't remember what we talked about for the rest of lunch. Afterwards, we did what we usually did and went back to my office off St Martin's Lane and made love on my couch. And yes, I'm afraid I have a casting-couch, though so far it has only ever entertained one man. I tried not to think about what James had told me, as we embarked on the familiar but ever-sweet engagement, but our post-student lovemaking had always been real, so after a bit we stopped and had a cup of tea instead and just looked out of the window at the church of St Martin-in-the-Fields. I suppose there must have been fields there once.

Later, when James had gone, I rang the National Gallery and asked if I could speak to someone who would tell me about the iconography of Aphrodite's hat. They put me through to a young man who was an art historian. He was very polite and began to tell me enthusiastically about the significance of Eros and the bees and how the son of the goddess of love had himself suffered from love's sting and how the 'hat' – he was especially polite about this – wasn't really a hat at all but – but suddenly I didn't want to hear and I gently pressed the receiver button as he was in full flow. He must have thought me rude; which I regret. I prefer not to be rude.

But I needed no longer to hear what anyone else thought or knew for I knew for myself why Aphrodite wore that hat. It wasn't mischief making. It was a recommendation to avoid total exposure. In case you give everything to someone who can't give it back.

'By all means go naked,' she seemed winningly to say, 'but keep your hat on . . .'

It's a magnificent hat. I have wished since I had one like it; or had been better able to learn from Aphrodite's example.

PRUNING

When Harriet Greenwald was cross she would often deal with it by gardening: vigorous digging, raking, mowing and – best of all – pruning usually put paid to any serious anger. Not that Harriet was essentially an angry person. She was, she liked to think, mostly easygoing. But, as everyone does, she had her moments. And these 'moments' tended to arise where her father was concerned.

Harriet's mother had departed life when her only child was sixteen. She had died under an anaesthetic during a quite ordinary procedure and Harriet had sometimes wondered if her mother had done it as a last resort, having tried, and failed, to leave her husband by less drastic means. Her mother had twice before attempted to escape the marital home: once in a solitary dash for liberty and once on the arm of the owner of a Turkish restaurant, who had promised the earth, or at least to provide for her in Tooting. But despite the restaurateur's forceful demeanour and material advantages – the restaurant had been doing well – the liaison had not been proof against the remedial effects of Harriet's father's disconcerting charm.

The charm, as charm generally is, was ephemeral. It emerged as a winning card on those occasions which Harriet's mother had used to call 'the last straw' (but which, due to the charm, never quite were). At other times, Harriet thought to herself as she savagely pruned swathes of the Virginia creeper which adorned their back wall, he was intransigent, selfish and crafty. He had been so today.

Harriet and her husband Mike were due to leave for the US at the end of the week to visit their daughter. Joanna had had an internship with a design studio in Boston specialising in sportswear. Despite the economic downturn, sportswear, it seemed, was booming and Jo had been taken on as an assistant designer.

Mike and Harriet were both teachers. It was over a year since they had seen their daughter and with the Easter holiday pending they had a splendid opportunity to pay her a visit. 'But,' Harriet had said grimly, 'before we make any serious commitment I'll have to be sure things are OK with Dad.'

Being sure things were 'OK' meant seeing to it

that her father did not alienate his latest carer, though how she was supposed to ensure such a thing, Harriet would dearly love to know. Mike said nothing to this. In the thirty-two years since his wife had died, his father-in-law had been a source of perpetual anxiety for his daughter, who was now the same age as her own mother when she finally escaped her husband's toils.

Over the last two years, Sam Davis had run through eight carers, all, as the agency assured in tones of reproach, coming with the highest recommendations. Four of the carers had been men, four women, so it was not gender discrimination operating as Harriet had hoped at first. Replacing the troupe of departed men with women had made not a blind bit of difference. Men and women alike, in the end Sam got them to go.

Nor was it any kind of racial prejudice. Her father had had British, Afro-Caribbean, Irish, Spanish, Polish and even Venezuelan carers. The fact was, whatever corner of the globe they hailed from, Sam Davis was always too much for them.

'What is it he does exactly?' Mike asked when the last-but-one carer had given notice.

Harriet reflected. Mike knew her father, so the question was rhetorical but it was worth trying to put a finger on it.

'He's changeable,' she said after a while. 'But not in the way that we all are. Deliberately. He muddles them: asks them to do things and then when they do just what he has asked he says, quite charmingly, that that wasn't what he wanted them to do, or that he never asked them to do it in the first place. It drives them mad. And it's not as though he has dementia or anything. He's perfectly sound in mind. He just likes to mess people about. It amuses him.'

'Yes, well it doesn't amuse me,' Mike had said. 'If he wasn't your dad and half paralysed, I'd thump him.'

'Someone will one day,' Harriet said. 'I don't know whether to dread it or pray for it.'

But today, cutting back the Virginia creeper, she was more inclined to the latter course.

All had been going so well. They had booked their tickets, suitcases were filling, Mike had Googled what to do in Boston and Harriet had found Jo's black silk camisole, without which, she emailed, she could no longer survive. And Mira, Sam's latest carer, seemed really to like him. When Harriet, her heart in her mouth, had visited last, she had found Mira sitting on the kitchen table eating chocolate digestives and screaming with laughter. It was true that what she was laughing at was a fiction with which Sam was regaling her about his alleged career in the navy. There were things about her father's life of which Harriet guessed she was ignorant, but that he was ever in the British navy she was pretty sure was not one of them.

But that very morning, just as everything looked set fair, Harriet received a call.

'Madam, I am sorry but I leave Mr Davis.' The sound of gentle crying filtered down the phone.

'Oh dear, Mira. Why? What has happened?'

'He ask me to buy him pyjamas and I buy and he send me back four times. Now he send me back to get the pyjamas I buy first. I say, "But these are what I bring in the first place." He say, "I know, I want to see again to see why I no like them." And then he hit my bottom. It is not right he do this, Mrs Greenwald. My behind it is not right he hit.'

'Mira, wait there. I'm coming right round.'

Mira let her in red-eyed. Harriet went straight through to the untidy garden room where she found her father sitting, apparently studying the sky. 'Dad, what's this I hear from Mira?'

Her father smiled in the way that to another person might have been winning. He waved his stick in the air. 'Have you ever studied clouds?'

'Dad, Mira says you hit her.'

'Good Lord.' Sam Davis turned a mild and mischievous stare on his daughter. 'As if I would.'

'She claims you smacked her bottom.'

Her father shrugged. 'The girl's an idiot. It was a mere affectionate pat.'

'Dad! For God's sake, this is the twenty-first century. You simply *can*not pat girls' bottoms.'

'Anyway, I've told her she must leave.'

'Why? We're about to go away.'

This, she saw, was a mistake. Her father's face took on a musing look. He was cooking up, Harriet suspected, an answer to rile her further. 'Have you considered the miracle of cloud formation?' he eventually asked.

'No,' Harriet said, furious. 'With a father like you I have more onerous things on my mind.'

Apologies and cajoling, and a couple of twenty-pound notes, failed to bring round Mira. She left, promising only, for Harriet's sake, or perhaps it was the twenty-pound notes, not to make any mention of the assault on her behind.

And now Harriet, clipping like mad at the already radically barbered Virginia creeper, was at a loss. Today was Saturday. On Maundy Thursday, she and Mike were due to fly to Boston, and what was to be done about her father? Social Services could of course be alerted but he had successfully alienated them long ago. And then, he had 'means'. Quite how much these 'means' amounted to, Harriet had never quite fathomed. But money it seemed was in too much supply for Social Services to consider a trying old man a real emergency.

The bell rang and, dismounting the ladder, Harriet went through the house to answer it.

Florid and smiling, Brenda Bottrell, the chairperson of the local gardening society, stood monumentally on the doorstep. 'The promised Hostas,' she announced, brandishing a bag overflowing with earthy foliage.

'Oh, thank you,' said Harriet, who had forgotten the chair had offered her these plants. 'Do come in,' she suggested, trying to make up for her forgetfulness, 'and have a cup of tea.'

'Well, maybe just the one.'

Mrs Bottrell, moving like a tank, manoeuvred herself on to the ricketiest kitchen chair. It was impossible not to suppose she had picked it deliberately as the least fit to bear her weight. Widowed for who knew how many years, Mrs Bottrell, Harriet had always to remind herself, must be lonely. Lonely but undeniably awful.

Over tea, Harriet explained that, regrettably, their impending Easter trip would mean her missing the next meeting of the garden society. Mrs Bottrell was condescending and understanding.

'I have never crossed the pond myself,' she averred, as if only the foolhardy failed to follow her example.

'Though we mightn't be going after all.' Harriet explained to Mrs Bottrell's questioning brow that her father's carer had given notice and she was pessimistic, at such short notice, about finding a replacement for the Easter weekend.

'Where does your poor father live?'

Electing not to query the 'poor', Harriet said, 'Just round the corner. We moved here to be near him when he had his stroke. He's half paralysed,' and sighed.

Mrs Bottrell's fierce little eyes took on a sudden lustre. 'If I can be of any help . . .? I *was*, you know, a trained nurse.'

It was as if some empress had loftily offered her services. 'Oh, I couldn't possibly impose,' said Harriet, flustered.

But later that evening, when the agency had 'regretted' they had 'no one at present suitable for Mr Davis', Mike said, 'Why not accept the old trout's offer? She might even enjoy it if time's heavy on her hands.'

'I doubt if anything is "heavy" on Mrs Bottrell's hands.'

None the less, the following morning Harriet rang the chair of the gardening society.

'If you really mean it,' Mike heard her say, 'then we will be for ever in your debt.'

Returning from Boston, Harriet delayed going round to her father's house longer than good conscience quite allowed. The trip had been heavenly. Jo was thriving and had a pleasant-seeming boyfriend, Mike had 'done' Boston and she had had time to catch up on her reading. On the few calls they had made to her father he had been uncharacteristically polite. Nevertheless, after bracing herself to ring to arrange the dutiful visit, it was with some trepidation that she walked up the path to his front door. The door, she observed, had been newly painted a startling red.

'Do come in.' Mrs Bottrell was gracious. 'Samuel is in the conservatory.'

Walking through to the garden room, Harriet saw that it was not merely the front door that had been radically altered but the familiar interior landscape of her father's house. The piles of old shoes, the shabby books and dusty prints were clean gone. The denuded walls were brilliant with paint and on a shelf, which had for ever held the *Encyclopaedia Britannica*, she observed a dimpling china shepherdess and her swain.

Her father's appearance had undergone a corresponding change. His formerly unkempt hair had been cut short, as, she detected, had his nails, which were unwontedly clean. Instead of the moth-eaten maroon pullover in which, for the past ten years, he had received her, he was sporting a crisp blue-and-white striped shirt beneath a navy blazer. His ancient slippers, she saw, looking down at his feet, had been replaced by a pair of smart brown brogues.

'He's looking better, isn't he.' It was an affirmation rather than a question. 'We've had a bit of a tidy since you've been gone.'

Harriet glanced at her father, expecting outrage. But with a shock, she saw his being was wholly focused on Mrs Bottrell, at whom he was gazing with adoring eyes. 'She's a marvel,' he exclaimed, turning finally to his daughter. 'Brenda is a marvel.'

'Get away, you old silly.' With a terrible mirthful jauntiness, Mrs Bottrell whacked Harriet's father in the region of what Harriet instinctively knew the Chair of the Garden Society would refer to as his 'backside'.

Harriet stared and Mrs Bottrell afforded her a majestic smile. 'He just needed a bit of pruning, didn't you, dear?' at which Harriet's father (as Harriet later told Mike) positively simpered. 'And there's no need to worry about "carers" any longer.' Mrs Bottrell waved a large manicured hand. 'Samuel and I got engaged. On Easter Sunday, actually,' she announced and, quite dreadfully, giggled. 'We are getting spliced as soon as we can. We were only waiting for you to come home, weren't we, Samuel?'

NIGHTMARE

somewhat blistered but still clearly and cleverly painted over with spiders and beetles and ladybirds – for Nan was quite an artist herself in her way. The shy little girl didn't cry one bit when her mother left her with their neighbour at number seven. Perhaps not enough, even, for Susannah's sense of her own importance to her daughter, though it went without saying that she was grateful for Nan's kindness.

When it was time for Kitty to start school, it made sense for Nan to collect her at the end of the day and give her her tea and keep the child round at hers until Susannah came home from work. And it made sense, too, that Kitty went to Nan's over half-term and in the school holidays. Kitty seemed not to miss her home or her parents during these periods and quite often spent the night in the brass bed, not quite a double but certainly wider than the usual single, which had once belonged to Nan's daughter, Bella, and then had been the province of Bella's twin girls. The twins were grown up now and had gone to New Zealand where one had married an oncologist and the other an ear, nose and throat specialist, keeping, as Nan liked to remark, on twin lines. On the head of the bed, Nan had painted a field mouse's nest with tiny curled field mice babies and beneath it, watching, a weasel with a predatory look in his black beads of eyes. These animals, the mouse family and the weasel, were among the cast of creatures woven into the stories which Nan told Kitty as she fell asleep on the nights her parents were out or it just seemed so much simpler for Kitty not to go home.

From time to time, Susannah worried about Kitty's attachment to Nan but Geoff would reassure her. 'She doesn't love us any the less for loving Nan,' he would say. 'Anyway, it's good for kids to have an extended family. Your parents are no use. Nor are mine, if it comes to that.'

Geoff's parents had been killed in an air crash before Kitty was born. Susannah had been born to her parents late in life and had been brought up on stern lines. She loved her daughter deeply, but the habits laid down in our childhood will noiselessly inform our adult behaviour and more of Susannah's parents' philosophy had rubbed off on her than she would have recognised or wanted to own.

One half-term holiday Kitty was staying over at Nan's and she had a nightmare. She got out of bed and ran to Nan's room where, hardly seeming to surface from unconsciousness, Nan had said soothingly, 'Hop in with me, pet, and snuggle down here.'

When she woke in the big bed which smelled of Nan's *Coty* talc, Kitty said, 'Mummy doesn't let me get into bed with them if I have nightmares.'

Nan said, 'Oh, there, Kitten. I'm sure she will if you ask her.'

Two days later Susannah called round to see Nan. After some awkward conversation about local events she said, 'Nan, Geoff and I want Kitty to learn to sleep alone. We'd prefer that when she stays here you don't allow her into your bed.'

Nan for a moment spoke her mind. 'That's cruel if the child is scared.'

Susannah's face took on the expressionless look of which Geoff, had he thought about it, had grown afraid. 'I don't want this to become an issue, Nan.'

The next time Kitty had a nightmare while staying at Nan's, Nan said, 'Go back to bed, darling,' and when Kitty began to wail piteously, 'Don't cry, my pet. I'll come and sit with you.'

Kitty, through tears, sobbed, 'But you let me last time . . .'

'I know, lovie.'

Nan sat by Kitty's bed till she fell asleep, her face still damp with tears. By then it was hardly worth going back to bed herself. She went downstairs and made a cup of tea and watched the dawn come up with a pain in her side.

After that, every time Kitty had a bad dream while staying at Nan's the child would beg to come into Nan's bed – and Nan, hating herself, refused. But one half-term, when Nan had not been feeling too good, and was too tired to keep up a protest she had in any case no belief in, she said, 'All right then, pet, hop in, but don't tell your mum or we'll both be in trouble.'

In the morning she said, 'Look, Kit. As far as

I'm concerned you can sleep where ever under God's heaven you like, but I have to do what your mum says.'

'Why?'

'I just have to, love.'

'I think she's silly.'

'No, she's your mum. We – that's you and I – have to do as she says.'

'I don't like her when she says things like that,' Kitty said.

By the time Kitty was eight years old, her open shyness had fallen away and her stand-offs with her mother were more frequent and sometimes nasty. One evening she shouted, 'I don't want to live with you any more, I want to live with Nan.'

'Well, you can't, you have to do as I say, young lady.' Susannah, who loved her daughter dearly, was wounded and retorted more sharply than she intended.

'I can, so.'

'No, you can't. While you're a child you have to do as I say.'

'It's not fair. I hate you,' Kitty yelled, rushing to her room and slamming the door. 'I only love Nan.'

Susannah was crying when Geoff came in from his studio. She told him what Kitty had said.

'Oh, Suzie, that's just kid's talk. Kit adores you.'

'No more than she adores Nan.'

'Nan's been kind to her. We've been glad enough when it suited us. Don't pick a fight, please.'

But next half-term Susannah arranged for her daughter to spend it with a friend.

Kitty went down the road to tell Nan. 'Mummy says I'm going for a sleepover with Flora.'

'That's nice,' Nan said. She had made a hazelnut cake, Kitty's favourite.

'She says I'm not coming here.'

'Never mind,' Nan said, comfortingly. 'There'll be other times.' When she understood that she was not going to see Kitty at all that half-term, she gave the tickets for the new Walt Disney film to the Garrod children over the road.

And somehow there were no 'other' times. With some difficulty, Susannah managed to organise different houses that her daughter could visit after school or over half-term, where she also spent nights when it was convenient. When Nan and Kitty met in the street they still hugged but no further occasion arose for Kitty to pass a night in the field-mouse bed.

One day, Kitty's teacher, Mrs Allen, asked if she could 'have a word'.

'Kitty's been a little off colour lately. Is everything all right at home?'

'I think so,' said Susannah, trying to pretend to herself that she had not been wondering about this too. 'What's the matter with her?' She had noticed that Kitty seemed strained and tired.

'She's not eating her school meals. And she's

getting into a few fights. Maybe it's just a bad patch. Children go through them, same as we do. I dare say it will pass.'

But a few weeks later Mrs Allen said, 'Mrs Giles, if you don't mind my asking, who is Nan?'

'A neighbour,' Susannah said. She didn't quite like to hear Nan's name.

'Kitty mentions her a lot. And she has written some stories. I just wondered quite what the relationship . . .'

'She used to fetch Kitty from school,' Susannah said.

'Did Kitty ever spend the night with her?'

'She used to,' Susannah said. She perhaps could not have explained why her tone had become defensive. 'But we've rather gone off the arrangement.'

'You know, I think that might be wise.'

Mrs Allen raised her pencilled eyebrows questioningly and Susannah, who had been feeling guilty about Nan, said in an effort to be fair, 'I don't think she was ever unkind to Kitty.'

Mrs Allen's frosted pink lipstick folded into a line. 'No. I'm sure. But that wasn't . . . I don't want to . . . but I wonder if there wasn't some sort of . . .'

'What?' Susannah asked, feeling rather frightened.

'I wouldn't say "abuse", because I don't say that it was anything overt, but Kitty writes a lot about their cuddles. It seems she sometimes slept with, er, Nan.'

That night Geoff said, 'Don't be ridiculous. My brother and I used to get into my parents' bed all the time. We often slept with them if we were ill – or had nightmares.'

'Geoff, we talked about that and we agreed. It was you as much as me.' Susannah was the more indignant for surmising that with another woman her easygoing husband would have been likely to accede to other terms for his child's sleeping arrangements.

'All I'm saying is that there is nothing sinister about Kitty's sleeping in Nan's bed. Until the Victorian period, everyone slept together: men, women and children. It was quite normal.'

He might have added that it is only humankind among the mammals who think it natural, and preferable, to sleep apart from their young.

Kitty looked anxious and then defiant when her mother explained that there was something she needed to ask.

'It's nothing horrible, darling, I promise. It's just about Nan.'

Kitty had grown wary of that word 'just'. It always seemed to bode so much more than implied. 'What about Nan?'

'When you slept in her bed –'

'I didn't.'

'Kitty, it is OK. We know you did. I only want to know what happened . . .'

'Nothing did.'

'Did Nan touch you?'

''Course she did. She cuddled me. We snuggled down together.'

'What did "snuggling" mean?'

Kitty looked at her mother in surprised scorn. 'Don't you know what "snuggling down" is?'

Two days later Nan received a note:

Dear Mrs Lethbridge,

We are grateful for all you have done for Kitty but for various reasons we feel the time has come to end the relationship. Kitty will not be coming to stay with you again. We should be grateful if you would not go out of your way to try to see her.

Your sincerely,

Susannah and Geoff Giles

At the end of the year, the Gileses moved house. Kitty needed a larger room, Susannah explained to Mrs Garrod over the road, when she met her in Tesco's. For some time, when Kitty had a nightmare she would comfort herself by imagining that she was safe and warm in Nan's large, soft, talc-scented bed. She knew better than to mention this to her mother. And after a longer while, because to do so was easier, Kitty forgot all about Nan.

THE GREEN BUS FROM ST IVES

William had not planned to go to St Ives over the May bank holiday. But four nights earlier, out of the blue, his wife, Helena, had announced that she was going to Paris with her friend, Dotty Blaine, adding casually that it would be 'all right about the dog and the cats' as William would be there 'to see to them'.

I'll be damned if I will, William had said to himself. As those who feel wronged will tend to, he searched about in his mind for something that would demonstrate his difference from his wife. He had never yet visited the Tate Gallery in St Ives and had been promising himself that pleasure for years. Helena didn't share his enthusiasm for modern art.

'I'm afraid I shall not be here,' he said, more

belligerently than he felt, for the truth was he felt rather scared. 'I'm going to St Ives.'

If Helena, who was used to her husband's mute acquiescence in her suddenly announced but often long-brooded plans, was surprised to hear of this proposal she didn't allow it to show. She was a woman who had worked to make efficiency her hallmark and she was not to be put out because her husband had taken it into his head to be mulish and awkward. She organised a neighbour to see to the cats and for Wanda, their cleaner, to walk Daisy the dachshund.

'I've given Wanda the number of the burglar alarm in case it goes off while we are away,' was all Helena said as she swept a carmine streak across William's cheek on her way out of the door to the taxi which was waiting to take her to Heathrow. She smelled, as always, delightful and William felt a flash of regret. But as his small act of rebellion seemed really not to trouble Helena he did not allow compunction to lessen his excitement.

So now he was on the train to Penzance, inwardly mouthing the Robert Louis Stevenson rhyme for children, *Faster than fairies, faster than witches* as they rushed through a countryside all green and white and yellow and alive with fields hopping with sturdy-looking lambs.

William had booked a room at a hotel he had found via the Internet. Privately he abhorred the

Internet, perhaps because Helena had become such a mistress of it. Their aged copy of *The Good Hotel Guide* had disappeared (no doubt considered by Helena redundant it had been passed on to a charity shop) and he was reluctant to give his wife rope by asking for her help. She would be sure to 'know' somewhere he 'must' stay. This trip, he had determined, was to be strictly his enterprise.

Arriving at Penzance, an almost violent smell of sea assaulted his nostrils. Above him a chaos of seagulls wheeled, white as angels, noisy and obstreperous as alley-cats. The hotel, painted a maritime blue, was easy to spot on the nearby rise. William was breathing hard by the time he had hauled himself and his suitcase up the cobbled incline. Not that he was a heavy man; on the contrary, he was slenderly built and fighting fit, he liked to think, for his years.

He was reassured by the hotel's peaceful interior: no sign of brass-work or Cornish piskies, a pleasing smell of wood smoke, elderly, well-polished furniture and white china jugs of pretty wild flowers. The young hotel manager showed him to his room.

'You're lucky, we had a cancellation so I put you in our best room. There's a view front and back, and you can see the weather from your bed.' The manager drew back the curtain to a chorus of screeching gulls. 'It looks set fair for the whole weekend.'

William hoped this was an omen and unpacked

his clothes. Unsure what to do next, he went out to explore Penzance.

It was the inconvenient time of day when – unless one is an alcoholic – it is too early for a drink and too late for tea. William bought a vanilla ice cream, licking it rather dubiously as he walked by the old harbour. It was one of those enjoyments, he decided, which are better in recollection. He had forgotten how ice cream will always drip down the cone and on to the wrist and sleeve, and was relieved when he finally polished the thing off.

What to do now? Had Helena been with him there would have been no problem filling the time. Already, she would have formulated plans for the day ahead and his part would have been merely to agree with or, less likely, dispute them. Over the long years of their marriage, the initiative had passed lock, stock and barrel to Helena. Suddenly a free man, he felt, as old recidivists are said to feel, nostalgic for familiar constraints.

He walked past a café which displayed in its window a timetable of the local bus service. Here was the chance to make some sort of plan. The bus to St Ives, he calculated, ran every forty minutes and took as long to get there. Well, that was good. He could set out tomorrow after breakfast and be in St Ives by ten.

There was a couple already in the hotel lounge when, after several consultations of his watch,

William felt it was decently possible to go down for a drink. The couple, expensively dressed, were sitting knit together on the more comfortable and capacious of the sofas. The girl had with her a vast patent leather handbag which she had placed on the coffee table so that it obscured William's view. Helena would have asked her to move it. Instead, William wished the couple good evening and asked if they had had a pleasant day.

The couple, who turned out to be Austrian, admitted that their day had passed well. But their demeanour indicated that this concession was to be the extent of their intimacy with him. They were there, their healthy young bodies suggested, for serious pleasure and were not about to squander their time in dull conversation with elderly men.

William took refuge in the dinner menu. Had Helena been there she would, by now, have been suggesting what he might like to order, forbidding certain dishes on health grounds and urging others on him for similar reasons. She herself would have chosen what was most likely to keep her figure the trim size 10 it had been since they had first met. Dover sole, probably, or perhaps the sea bass. William found it was easier to guess what Helena might have eaten than to choose for himself.

Dinner was just himself and the amorous Austrian couple, who had taken off their shoes and were playing footsie under the table. William ate his lamb in silence. He thought wistfully of Daisy and felt envious of Wanda walking her in the park.

Over coffee, he chatted to the young hotel manager, more for a need to demonstrate to the Austrians that he was capable of being good company than for any inclination to talk. He confided his project of visiting St Ives. The manager said that it was possible to hire a car from Dave's down the road but that if he were William he would take the local bus; the parking in St Ives was dreadful and the traffic tomorrow would, he could guarantee, be nobody's business.

William, in fact, had already decided on the bus, but he was grateful for the manager's advice. His wish to oblige was such that he might have felt compelled to hire one of Dave's cars had the manager recommended it. Politeness, as Helena never tired of assuring him, was William's bane.

Despite the large dimensions and even larger softness of the bed, William slept poorly. He dreamed and woke with a start but with no recollection of the dream. Getting out of bed, he went to the window and drew back the curtains. Moonlight was playing in a trembling dance over black water. The masts of the boats made a stack of black spillikins topped with an occasional white blur of resting birds.

William got back into bed, turned on the side-light and tried to read his book. But it was no good.

For the life of him he couldn't take in what he was reading. He switched off the light and lay in the sea-lit darkness, wondering about Helena. Was she sharing a room in Paris with Dotty Blaine and if so did they lie and chat together at night, as he and Helena had done in the past? He remembered a time when they were students, lying in someone's loft in sleeping bags, side by side but with their cocooned bodies touching, talking through the night till the birds rang in the morning. He would not be sure what to talk to her about now.

He was very early at the bus stop, a habit for which Helena mocked him and he felt the relief of being allowed to indulge his anxiety free of any critical comment. Over the years, he could not help having noticed, his wife had grown to the opinion that her husband was a poor fish. Well, perhaps she was right, he thought, stepping on to the bus which had now pulled up and was letting aboard a queue of impatient passengers.

William found a seat towards the back of the bus. Behind him, two American women seated themselves and, as they got underway, became enthusiastic and voluble about the Cornish countryside.

'See there, Janie, those lambs. They might be out of a nursery rhyme.'

Janie, it seemed, was made of sterner stuff than her companion. She remarked that the same lambs were very likely bound for the butcher's block, adding that the lamb they had had last evening at the restaurant had been as sweet as butter.

Her travelling companion was silent on this topic but kept her end up by trying to recall a children's rhyme. '*As I was going to St Ives, I met a man with seven wives* . . . but I can*not* remember how it goes on, Janie.'

William turned around. '*Seven wives had seven cats, seven cats had seven kits, kits, cats, men, wives, how many were going to St Ives?*' he quoted.

The woman who was not Janie beamed. 'That's it. How very kind of you.'

Janie had been calculating. 'Twenty-two.'

Her companion laughed, exalted but nervous that she was about to best her friend. 'No, the answer's one. You see he *met* the man with all the wives. He, the man with the wives, I mean, was coming from St Ives, it's the speaker who is going there.'

But Janie was not to be contradicted. 'Why shouldn't he meet them on the way? He might be overtaking the guy if he had all those blessed creatures to drag along with him.'

It was the sort of remark Helena might have made. William turned back to observe the countryside. The fields were not, as they had seemed from the window of the train, merely yellow and white but pink and blue besides. He wished he knew more about wild flowers. He had picked up a little about the garden ones over the years from Helena. Helena, as she liked to say, was 'dedicated' to her garden.

Reaching St Ives, the bus came to a faltering halt on the brow of the hill. Fearful that Janie and her companion might latch on to him, William set off purposefully down the crowded streets towards the wide curved sandy bay where the St Ives Tate stands.

His visit to the gallery took up most of the morning. He was looking at a drawing of roof-tops by Ben Nicholson when he noticed a tall young woman, dressed in jeans and boots, entering the room. She was not particularly good-looking but her face was interesting. It was long and pale and bony, the sort of face, William speculated, that an artist might like to draw.

The girl came across and stood beside William, looking at the clean line of the roof-tops until he half thought of addressing her. But as he was considering what he might say she wandered off and out of the room.

William, watching her leave the room, found that he was hungry. He walked downstairs and out of the gallery and went in search of lunch. He followed the narrow road till he found a small place, not too crowded, advertising homemade soups and salads. He was eating a ham salad when the tall girl with the bony face came into the café. Involuntarily, he smiled at her.

The girl looked at him, frowning slightly. The

119

tables were crammed together and he expected her to take a distant one but she came and sat at the table nearest his, almost touching his arm. 'You were in the Tate this morning.'

'That's right,' William said, pleased at having been noticed.

'You were looking at the Ben Nicholson.'

'Yes,' William agreed. And, 'I like Nicholson,' he offered.

The girl nodded as if that were an accepted fact between them. 'Looking at pictures makes me hungry. You too?' Her voice was deepish with an accent, hard to place, but he guessed from somewhere North.

'I suppose it does. I'd not thought.'

'Well,' the girl said, 'me, I'm ravenous.'

'Where are you from?' William risked after she had ordered.

'Derbyshire. The Peak District.'

'Like Joseph Wright. You've come a long way.'

'Too right,' said the girl. She was eating bread ferociously, tearing it into chunks and cramming it into her mouth. She spoke now through the bread, 'How about you?'

'Oh, nowhere interesting,' William apologised. 'London.' He wondered whether to offer her the contents of his own, still full, breadbasket.

'London's good,' the girl said, ripping into more bread. 'You shouldn't knock London.'

William, who had meant to be reassuring, felt put in his place. The girl turned her attention to her chicken salad. This too she wolfed down, eating so fast that by the time William was ready to order coffee her plate was clean and she was ordering coffee with him. 'You having a sweet?'

William who never ate cake and rarely pudding said, 'Maybe I'll try a flapjack.'

'Go on. A little of what you fancy . . .'

I fancy you, William thought to himself and all but blushed. 'I try to watch my calories,' he explained.

'Don't look as if you need to,' the girl said, sinking her teeth into the slice of walnut cake the waitress had brought. The girl's teeth were large and even. She reminded William of a hungry horse.

He said, for something to say, 'Do you know the rhyme about St Ives?'

'Don't think so. Tell me.'

When he'd recited it she thought a moment and frowned again and said, 'It's one, isn't it?'

'It's not very difficult,' he apologised, and told her about the bus and Janie.

'Yeah, well, you know those old American girls.'

Pleased to be exempted from the category of being 'old', when the bills arrived he asked, summoning courage, 'May I give you lunch?'

'You mean pay for mine?'

There was no other way of putting it. 'Yes.'

121

'Ta. That's kind.'

'Not at all,' William said, relieved to have done the right thing. She might be a feminist and object to being patronised.

They walked back together up the steep cobbles towards the Tate. William, looking down at the girl's sturdy boots and his own neatly polished brogues, wondered how he could keep her at his side. Suddenly she said, 'Let's go to Trewyn Studio, shall we?' and when he turned to her a surprised face, explained, misconstruing his expression, 'You know, Barbara Hepworth's place.'

'*Finding Trewyn Studio was a sort of magic.*' William read aloud the words from the informative leaflet provided by her studio. They had passed out of the buildings and through into the garden and were standing under the shade of trees through which the clear May sunlight was dappling the dead sculptor's monumental creations of stone and wood and bronze.

'It *is* magic,' said the girl. 'Like an enchanted place.' She swayed a little and William took her arm.

'Are you all right?'

'Never better. It's just, all this . . .' She swept out a large, almost mannish hand, to indicate the vista before them. The hand, he couldn't help noticing, bore the marks of several cuts. 'It's too much.' There were tears in her voice and, turning

122

his gaze, he saw the visible counterparts glimmering in her eyes.

'I don't know your name,' he said, embarrassed. Helena would never have cried in a public place like that.

'Hazel. What's yours?'

'William. Like your eyes,' he added.

But this she chose to ignore. Perhaps he had offended her. I must be careful, he thought. Me an old man with this young thing.

'You know how Hepworth died?' the girl asked. They had returned to the studio and were looking at a naked torso carved in stone. It might, William thought, resemble the girl's. Although he did know of the tragedy that had killed the famous sculptor, he let the girl explain. 'She burned to death in her own studio. They think it must have been a faulty wire.'

'Horrible.' He shook his head, unable to begin to imagine anything so awful. The terror of it, the pain.

'But at least her work survived. She would have been glad about that.'

He had a sudden inspiration about the cuts on her hands. 'You're a sculptor, too?'

'I try.'

'But that's marvellous.'

'It doesn't really keep the wolf from the door. But it's what I want to do.'

'Oh, always do what you want to do, my dear.' In his admiration for what he saw as her brave choice of life, he slapped his new companion on the shoulder harder than he had intended. Once more she swayed and seemed almost to crumple. 'Look,' he asked, concerned now, 'are you really all right?'

'I'm just tired. I slept on a bench last night. Lucky it was warm.'

'You had nowhere to go?'

She laughed, showing the strong teeth untarnished by age. 'I hadn't the money, guv.'

'Oh Christ,' he said. 'I'm sorry to be so tactless.'

'You couldn't know. I was saving it for this – and for a decent lunch, as a treat. So, thanks to you buying me lunch I've got some extra now to spend.'

Walking down the hill towards the bus stop William wondered how he could put to her what was in his mind. He had a horror of seeming to patronise such vivid independence. And he was aware of his own neediness, the loneliness and the attendant wish to extend the time spent with her, which might not – almost certainly wouldn't – be to her liking. Nearing the bus stop, he asked, 'Where are you going?' and was relieved when she said, 'Penzance.' So they could travel together and he could postpone what he wanted to say – what he thought, at least, he wanted to say. On the bus, he could reconsider if he wanted to make his bold suggestion – that the girl take a room for the night at the hotel, at his expense, of course. An image assailed him of the amused ironical smile Helena would give if she were privy to this proposition.

The bus was already revving up to leave when they reached the bus stop. A green bus, almost full up with its complement of passengers. One seat only was free as if it were waiting especially for them.

The bus started off as soon as they had boarded and began to make a brisk progress through St Ives. William sat, rather more upright than was quite comfortable, conscious of the girl's body beside him. In his mind's eye he couldn't help seeing again the Hepworth torso, beautiful in its lean grace. All of a sudden, the bus lurched violently and then took off at a terrific lick. They drove through the outskirts of the small town, careering around corners as the passengers were tossed wantonly about in their seats. Reaching, finally, the freedom of the wider main road the driver accelerated wildly.

No one on the bus seemed to make anything of this but William and the girl. Surely, though, they asked each other, ruminating cattle and quietly grazing sheep must have recognised, as they rattled past, a madman? At first bemused, then entertained and finally laughing fit to bust William and the girl clutched each other as they were jolted back and forth. There was no question now of William avoiding the girl's body. For safety's sake, they clung together for dear life.

The strange thing was, they agreed, finally alighting at Penzance, arm in arm like drunks with tears of laughter still in their eyes – yes, the strange thing was how the other passengers sat quite placidly through it all. As if they were quite accustomed to being driven by a maniac.

'My God,' she said. 'What was that about? What was he about, the driver?'

They were walking along the harbour front, still laughing, still a little shocked and excited. 'Look,' William said, 'I'm staying up there, at that hotel, see.' He waved towards the beacon of blue on the rise. 'How about a drink to celebrate our survival?'

'I wouldn't mind.'

William felt proud as he escorted the girl into the hotel lounge. The Austrians had taken up position on the larger, deeper sofa, so William and Hazel had no option but the smaller, less accommodating one. But in their recent escapade William's anxiety over physical proximity had evaporated. His shoulder now touched the girl's companionably as side by side, like colleagues, they drank their gin and tonics. They were still under the enchantment of their adventure – a fact which William presently saw was making the Austrians suspect that it was they who were being laughed at.

Concerned not to seem rude, he attempted explanation. 'We're laughing because we've just had a most extraordinary nightmare ride.'

'Excuse me. Nightmare ride?' the man of the couple solemnly enquired, which set Hazel off again into great whoops of laughter.

'I'm sorry,' she said when the Austrians, with a marked Prussian stiffness, had made their way out of the lounge and through to the dining room and she and William were alone. 'But they looked so offended and it was nothing to do with them.'

'It takes a large heart not to take things personally,' William said, surprising himself, for he had not known that he knew this.

'Oh, I do agree.' The hazel eyes were looking levelly at his. He thought, She has candid eyes.

'Listen,' he said, touching her sinewy forearm. How well he could envisage it welding steel or sawing wood. 'Would you do me the honour of accepting my hospitality? If there's a room free here tonight, will you let me give it you? A kind of –' he hesitated, he didn't want to seem to be offering to thank her for her company exactly – 'acknowledgement', he alighted on, 'of our shared experience of the green bus from St Ives.' For all his newfound confidence he was careful to make it clear that it was a room separate from his own one that he was offering her.

She continued to look at him, not warily but with the same frank look in her eyes.

'You know what,' she said at last. 'That's kind. Very kind. I accept.'

'Really?' Now he had pulled it off he felt the risk he had taken with his odd gesture – the risk of offending her, of clouding the immense fun they had had, were still having.

'Really.' She nodded, smiling at him, her eyes still quite at ease.

'And dinner?'

'Yeah, dinner too. But not here. That would make me feel guilty. Too pricey.' She took his arm. 'Come on. Let's find the local chippy.'

'Let's get you that room first.' He would have gone with her to McDonald's had she suggested it.

He was sleeping dreamlessly when he was woken by the tapping at his door. 'What is it?' For a moment, he could not recall where in the world he was.

'It's me. Can I come in?'

He was out of bed in a trice and putting on the light and his dressing gown. 'What time is it? Are you all right?'

'You keep asking that,' she said. 'I thought it would be nice to talk.'

'Of course, but where . . .?' He looked round the room vaguely as if the hotel might have made some special provision for this unlooked for event.

'In bed, stupid.'

'Oh. Right ho, then.'

128

He got back into bed, still in his dressing gown.

'Aren't you going to be hot in that?' She was wearing a long cotton T-shirt. Nothing more.

'I thought you would rather . . .'

'Don't be silly.' By now she was in the bed beside him. 'I would have been happy to share. I thought that's what you had in mind.'

But at this he protested. 'Oh no. I never thought you'd . . .'

'Don't worry, it's not for ever and ever amen. Just tonight. So we remember the bus ride.'

In the morning she said, 'I'm catching an early train. Don't argue, the ticket's booked and I can't change it. But this here –' handing him a leaflet – 'is about an exhibition I'm showing some work at soon. Come and visit me if you fancy seeing it.'

William was back home and reading in the sitting room with the larger tortoiseshell cat on his knee when Helena returned from Paris. She sailed in, bearing a flat white box which when opened revealed some exquisite cherry tarts.

'How was your arty trip?' She kissed him graciously, still smelling gorgeous, not, in truth, wanting to know.

'Immense fun.'

'Really?' Helena raised her perfectly symmetrical eyebrows. William could usually be counted on to have a dull time.

'Really. I found a pleasant hotel. Next time you go off on one of your jaunts I might go away again.'

Helena's scarlet mouth made the slightest movement of resistance. 'If the hotel's that good, then perhaps I'll come too.'

'I don't think it's your cup of tea. I had to have supper in the local fish and chip shop and there was a traumatic bus ride from St Ives. I doubt I shall ever recover.' He hoped he never would.

'Food in the hotel no good?'

'Not in the circs, no.'

'Doesn't sound much fun to me.' She glanced at the book. 'What are you reading?' She never usually asked.

'It's about modern sculpture.' He closed the book, marking his place with a leaflet. He nodded down at it. 'There's an interesting exhibition coming on in Derbyshire. I might go.'

Helena gave a dramatic shiver. 'Derbyshire? Brrrr. Chilly.'

'Yes,' said William, comfortably. 'I know. That wouldn't be your cup of tea either.'

THE SPHINX

'Did you know that Sphinx means "strangler", and that she strangled travellers who couldn't solve her riddles?' Sylvie Armstrong asked a fellow guest during a dull conversation about Egypt at a dinner party.

'I wonder how the bodies were disposed of?' was the rejoinder.

Sylvie was impressed. The young man seated beside her was beautiful and she had asked the question expecting a more sentimental response.

Sylvie's husband, Phillip, whose son was an archaeologist out on a dig in Egypt and had raised the topic under discussion, shot a look across the table. She knew that look. It meant: please don't embarrass me in public.

'She ate them, I think,' Sylvie continued. 'Though

they never explained the "whys" of that sort of thing, did they, the ancients? I mean, why would one mind so much if one's riddles remained unanswered?'

'Perhaps it was disappointment,' was the young man's response to that. 'Maybe she didn't know the answers herself and strangled them in frustration when they failed to come up to expectation.'

A psychoanalyst who had been lecturing the rest of the table on the manifestations, late in life, of addiction to the breast, shoved his oar in at that point. Perhaps it had to do with an infantile fear of being smothered by the placenta at birth? he suggested, somewhat aggressively bringing up the Oedipus complex. But Sylvie was too intrigued by her young man to be led into the misty labyrinth of psychoanalytic theory.

'I expect you're right.' Her eyes covertly surveyed his across the table. He had, she noted, the mild china-blue eyes of a certain breed of expensive cat. 'But you can't help wondering why someone so powerful needed someone else to supply them with answers.'

'It is of the essence of power,' the young man equably suggested, 'to look for a match.'

'And ditch it when it proves unequal . . .?' Sylvie asked.

Although Sylvie found her husband tiresome she had never been unfaithful to him. Infidelity was not her line. She didn't like complications and sex with anyone but her husband was something she was prepared to try again only in the unlikely event that she might fall in love. She had been in love once and the experience had been painful. The other person had been married and they had agreed to be honourable. In marrying Phillip, she had succumbed to the lure of security – a false one, as she now saw, but the nature which had kept her from stealing another woman's man also kept her faithful. So when the beautiful young man telephoned at first she pretended not to know who he was.

'Who is it?' she enquired. And waited.

'If that's a riddle it's either very difficult or very easy,' was the answer. And after that Sylvie stopped pretending with Jamie Ransome.

Sylvie had always thought of herself as someone who disliked the phone. 'I can't think what we find to say to each other,' she remarked one day when Jamie had called three times.

'We speak the things we would otherwise say only to ourselves,' he replied.

There was no doubt that it was flattering to be the object of so much attention from someone so young and so beautiful.

'I am eighteen years older than you, old enough to be your mother,' Sylvie commented when Jamie exclaimed that a particular hairstyle made her look sixteen.

'An indecently young mother,' was his rejoinder, 'and besides, a person's "age" has more to do with their soul than their chronological years.'

Sylvie had worried at first that she might fall in love with Jamie; it hardly seemed possible she could avoid doing so. It was not so much his beauty but the wisdom of his utterances which she found compelling. To be understood was a secret yearning; one she had put away after the experience of falling in love had worked out so badly. Phillip understood her so little that it was almost a relief. There was a cool privacy in his non-comprehension which left her free to be herself. But to be oneself is almost always lonely; to be perceived and apparently comprehended was unexpected, and disarming.

Sylvie hoped that she was not going to make a fool of herself, something, temperamentally, she fought shy of. But as the weeks went by, and she and Jamie became more and more familiar, she was glad to note that while she occasionally wanted to fold him in her arms, she had no thoughts of any greater intimacy with her new friend. Instead, they talked, animatedly, and intimately, several times a day, and went on shopping trips together, where Jamie dictatorially chose her clothes and issued decrees over makeup.

From time to time, Sylvie wondered what Phillip made of her friendship; but a bonus of living with Phillip was his apparent indifference to how his wife spent her time. That she might be becoming a little dependent on Jamie occasionally troubled her. But she was not a dependent sort and told herself firmly that when, as she must expect, Jamie found more enthralling company than herself she would swallow any hard feelings and be dignified.

However, Jamie seemed to want no other confidante and, after a while, she began to take her position with him for granted. The dinner they had met at was in February. 'We'll have known each other six months next week,' she reminded him. The six months had passed in the blink of an eye. She could not say where the time had gone; only that it had passed more vividly than usual.

'We must celebrate,' Jamie declared. 'We'll put on our glad rags and paint the town red. Where would you like to go?'

Before he went off to be killed in the Great War, Sylvie's grandmother had met the love of her life at Claridge's and it lingered in Sylvie's mind as the most desirable place in London to dine. She and Jamie were not a romance, they were something else – unique, as he was always saying – but nevertheless, she felt almost timid when she suggested the celebrated hotel as a possible venue for their own celebration.

'It's rather luxurious,' said Sylvie – which was not like her. On the whole she took for granted the fact that luxury was her due.

'Don't be absurd,' said Jamie. 'For people like us no corner should be cut.'

Sylvie spent an unusual amount of time shopping to buy her outfit for the celebration evening. She found the experience enervating. Unconsciously, she had come to rely on Jamie's decisive judgement over what suited or didn't suit and deprived of this firm touchstone she found herself unusually dithery and at sea.

In the end, she bought a dove-grey frock, a smart pink suit and a little black dress, to add to the many similar ones already accumulated in her wardrobe. She arrived home fatigued, with quantities of bulky carrier bags, to a brief message from Phillip on the answer phone.

'Hugh's back from Egypt. He'll be arriving this evening.'

Hugh was Phillip's son by his previous marriage. Sylvie had tried her best with Hugh, but the relationship had remained strained. Hugh was an only child; his mother was a confirmed hypochondriac who, despite the fact that the marriage had ended long before the advent of Sylvie, made it plain that the source of any continuing infirmity was the usurping second wife.

Sylvie rang Phillip. 'I'm out tonight – what do you want me to do about Hugh?'

'I'll be tied up till late,' was the unpromising answer. 'Can't you cancel?'

'No,' Sylvie said, 'I can't.'

Phillip's obliviousness to her arrangements was matched by a blank insistence over his own which angered and occasionally depressed Sylvie when she came up against it. 'You'll have to organise something – I can't get back and he's no key.'

'I can leave a key with Marje.' Marje was their cleaner. But, no, she couldn't, she remembered: Marje was off with her sister for a week in Lanzarote. 'Can't he get here before I leave?'

'I don't know when he'll turn up,' said Phillip. 'I told him you'd be in. I'm sorry, I've a meeting to get to now.'

Sylvie tried on the dove-grey dress, disarranged her hair as she pulled it off again, smudged mascara on the pink silk suit, snagged her tights as she changed them for a second time and finally settled for the little black number, not the new one, but another she'd had in the wardrobe unworn for an age. She settled down with a large gin and tonic to wait for Hugh and tried to calm herself. A part of her suspected that Hugh knew about the dinner and sensed that it was important to her: he had the uncanny intuitive flair of the ill-disposed.

At ten to eight, Sylvie, defying burglars, left a note on the door. 'Will be at Claridge's. Come there for key.' She did not quite dare to defy Phillip enough to leave Hugh wholly abandoned.

The taxi she called at the last minute was late, and by the time they reached their destination the evening had turned humid and she was sweating in the little black number which appeared to have acquired moth holes in the skirt. She almost lost the third pair of tights as a woman in killer heels nearly trod on her foot as she hurried from the taxi.

But there to greet her in the cool, dimly lit dining-room was a welcoming Jamie, kissing her cheeks and commenting appreciatively on her scent – 'Chanel 22, no?' – as he helped her with attentive hands to her seat at their carefully placed table.

She had chosen her starter, and was laughing in relief at his wicked observations over a very cross couple dining in silence at the other side of the room, when she heard a voice behind her.

'Jay!'

'Hugh!' Across the table, the opaque cat's eyes she knew so well were alight with a strange feverish fire.

'What are you doing here?'

'I'm dining with a friend, Sylvie Armstrong. Sylvie – my very, very old friend Hugh . . .'

Sylvie found herself tongue-tied during dinner. The conversation about Hugh's Egyptian dig dominated the evening and it was late when Jamie called her a cab. He brushed her cheek and thanked her for the 'enjoyable evening' and promised to be 'in touch' in the next few days.

Sylvie was still up drinking when Phillip arrived home. He asked for Hugh and she delivered the message. 'He sends his love and says to tell you not to worry. He ran into an old friend – he'll be staying with him for a while.'

THE INDIAN CHILD

(for Samuel Raphael)

'But what, beyond the world, does she want with a human child?' the visitor enquired.

'His mother was a votaress of her order,' Rowan explained.

The explanation struck her, as she voiced it, as lame. The connection hardly seemed strong enough to justify the scenes which had raged over the little Indian boy whose mother, a friend of the queen's, had died in childbirth.

'One of your idle fancies, acting the saviour,' the king had chided. A pretty poppet, at least by mortal standards, Rowan thought, but no match for the queen's terrible beauty or the king's awe-inspiring features. The plainest of us, she considered as she eyed the visitor, is more remarkable than the round-eyed dust-coloured man child. And yet the queen doted on him, still took him into her bed at night wrapped in costly Indian shawls – the only surviving relics of his mother – and played with him each morning, quite as if she were a mortal and he her own offspring.

'I wonder what the child makes of it all?' The visitor was of the king's party but had long ago given up taking sides except to convey the appropriate official demonstrations of loyalty. From time immemorial, the two households had been an unstable liaison, sometimes at it hammer and tongs and then, as suddenly, falling into recapitulations of old affections, only to set off again before long on some new quarrel. It made him weary to think of it. Truly, immortality was a doubtful blessing. 'Mind if I take a look at the boy?' he asked.

Rowan frowned. 'What for?'

'Interest only,' the visitor said nonchalantly. 'In all this time I've not set eyes on him and naturally one becomes curious.'

Since the child was in the next room, it was an easy matter to grant the request. Rowan had rather warmed to the visitor. Her own order of males were a dull lot – pansies and dragonflies – and she was, without knowing why, attracted by the sense of simmering danger the visitor had about him.

She moved towards the door behind them and opened it warily, for in exposing the boy to potential predators she was disobeying orders.

A flight of stairs ran down to a high-vaulted room. At its centre a young boy squatted, his glossy head bent. He was drawing something on the sandy floor and seemed wholly absorbed.

'Manu,' Rowan called. 'We have a guest. Come and say hello.'

The boy got up and padded towards them. He had, the visitor thought, for a mortal an expression of considerable calm. He extended a long silvery hand to the child.

Manu held out his own plump brown one in return and bowed his head slightly. 'I am delighted to meet you,' he said gravely.

The visitor also bowed. 'Likewise. You are well?'

'I am well,' said the little boy, 'if a little bored.' He spoke with a pure diction as if, which was not exactly the case, this was not his own tongue.

The visitor turned to Rowan and raised his eyebrows. 'Bored, is it?'

'Are you, Manu?' she asked, a little flustered. The child had shown no previous signs of discontent.

'Oh, always to be safe and happy is dull,' the child announced. As if to demonstrate the truth of these words, he took off, sprinting away round the large room with his arms held wide and beating the air. 'I can't fly,' he announced, coming to rest before the visitor.

'No one flies here,' Rowan said, embarrassed.

The visitor looked sideways at her with narrow sloe-blue eyes. 'But we can if we choose,' he murmured.

'But,' said Rowan flustered still more, 'it is thought . . .'

'Vulgar?' the visitor suggested and laughed, showing two double rows of pointed yellow teeth.

There was something disturbing in this which made Rowan move protectively towards the boy who was gazing up at the visitor entranced. 'Can you fly?' he asked.

'Oh, we all can,' the visitor, whose name was Monkshood, replied. 'But it's not done.'

'Why not?' The upturned face, which still showed traces of childish pudginess, had the look of a being far older – a Buddha maybe.

'Lord knows,' said Monkshood. 'Etiquette is always obscure in observance and hard to explain. The lower orders fly, of course. But among our kind . . .' he waved a mauve-veined hand at the end of which the nails curved dangerously.

'I would like to fly,' Manu stated.

'Ah,' said the visitor, now a little bored himself. 'I dare say.'

It was in fact about the boy that Monkshood had come. He had been sent as an ambassador from the king to reopen the negotiations for the child to be sent across to his kingdom. Monkshood was a practised diplomat but he was obliged to admit that so far they had got nowhere. Quite why it was that both these powerful beings had such a passion to have this child under their sway was beyond his understanding. Seeing the boy in the flesh had made Monkshood none the wiser. The brat was attractive enough, to be sure, for a human; but there was nothing obviously special about him. As the boy himself had remarked, he couldn't even fly, as the meanest of their kind could.

However, Monkshood was there to further the king's business, not to question its merits. He adjusted his usually unforthcoming expression to one of sincere but mild appeal. He knew he had been chosen as the emissary least likely to irritate the queen.

'Your majesty,' he said, bowing low on entering her presence. 'It is most gracious of you to agree to see me amid so many more pressing demands.'

The queen slightly inclined her neck. They both knew that she had nothing to do since all the usual activity within her province was on hold while the dispute over the child seethed. 'Gracious is as gracious does. What is it you have come to ask?' As if I didn't know, her manner as good as added.

'Your majesty, it is the usual request. You have heard it many times. Too many times, I sometimes fear.' Monkshood judged that a slight disloyalty towards the king was worth the risk of his displeasure should he hear of it.

The queen smiled. It was a cold smile and might

have brought goose flesh to a human skin. To Monkshood, however, it was moonshine on water.

'Quite so. Your king is well acquainted with my views. His mother was a votaress of my order; and, in the spiced Indian air, by night, full often has she gossiped by my side; and sat with me on Neptune's yellow sands.'

The queen looked dead at Monkshood with long eyes that had darkened to a forbidding black. 'But she, being mortal, of that boy did die. And for her sake do I rear up her boy and for her sake I will not part with him.'

Monkshood sighed. It was as he had predicted. But it was his duty to have one more try. 'Is there nothing you can give me to tell the king that will give him hope?'

'Nothing,' said the queen. 'I am afraid you must return to your king empty of words of comfort.'

Manu had been taken from the human world before he was a day old, but he was perfectly aware that he was a mortal boy. He was not a changeling – that is a child who has been swapped at birth for a fairy child. He was an orphan who had been abducted by the queen perhaps out of her much-vaunted love for his mother or perhaps, as the queen's consort had snidely suggested, as a mere fancy. That she was prone to fancies Manu, who was a quick child, was well aware.

Since he could remember, she had taken him into her bed to cuddle and caress him but these days he preferred to be put to his own bed by Rowan, the queen's lady-in-waiting. Rowan was relatively young. Not that anyone could ever determine a fairy's exact age, since fairies evolved, rather than being born, in a process somewhat like the life-cycle of plants – moving from seed to husk immensely slowly over aeons of time yet never dying. The queen, he knew, was very old, even for a fairy. Her consort was slightly younger by a couple of thousand years. This information could not have been gleaned from their appearance, which never altered; or, if it did, so gradually that no mortal reckoning could register the change.

Manu had no absolute measure of his own age but over the years, when he could escape the vigilance of his carers, he had been in the way of finding a route from the thick of the wood to its verge, where human children sometimes came to play. Most often, it was the wilder boys who ventured there. They came in excited trepidation since there were still wild animals which, at times of dearth, would come foraging and were capable of savaging a child or even eating one alive. Manu crouched in trees above the playful children's heads, concealed by his dark skin and the capacity learned of his adopted kind for camouflage, watching fascinated the mortal children. From these forays, he had worked out that he must now be about the age of the older boys, which was ten or eleven years old.

It was hardly possible for him not to be aware that he was the subject of a struggle between the queen and king. The king having at first indulged the queen over the adoption had conceived a fancy for her mortal prize himself and had demanded Manu be handed over to become his henchman. But the queen had consistently refused to surrender up her charge. In consequence, all the seasonal workings of nature, in correspondence with their rulers, had been at loggerheads: roses bloomed in snow, birds built their nests in fog and ice, and the whole natural world was topsy-turvy and in stasis.

Manu, suspecting that the arrival of the visitor had something to do with this dispute, had followed the ambassador to the queen's quarters and had seen him emerge with an expression that suggested that his mission had failed.

'Excuse me,' the boy said, approaching. 'May I talk to you?'

That same evening Monkshood spoke to the king.

'That there was no joy from her majesty will hardly surprise you, sir, but I did meet the boy and we conversed.' The king's expression brightened, but he waited for his ambassador to continue. 'He has conceived a desire to fly. I explained this is hardly possible.'

'But he wishes to learn?'

'So it seems.'

'Ah,' said the king, 'then perhaps we are in business.'

As a frail moon lifted itself above the darkening trees the king set out, unattended. He made these solitary excursions from time to time. Unlike the queen, his nature craved occasional solitude. Moving soundlessly over the dense undergrowth, he arrived at his destination, a circle of birches enclosing a patch of grass silvered by the wasted moon. But the glade was not, as the king had been expecting, unpeopled, for leaning against the peeling white trunk of one of the trees sat a shape.

The king moved swiftly back into the night shadows but the shape stirred and resolved into the figure of a person who spoke to him.

'Well met, your majesty.' So he was one of those that could see. He must then be a halfling, that is a mortal with a degree of fairy genes. 'Forgive me if I am trespassing on your territory,' the mortal continued. For all his respectful address, he appeared quite at ease at the encounter.

'Not my territory,' the king said, moving into the moonlight.

'Perhaps, then, your wife's?'

'She is not my wife.' The king, who felt caught out, spoke with a certain chilly stiffness.

'I beg your pardon. Your –' the mortal broke

151

off, conveying that he lacked the proper term.

'My queen,' the king offered, more amicably.

'Indeed, your queen,' the mortal agreed.

'I came here,' the king began and halted. He was visited by an odd inclination to confide in this halfling but his customary hauteur held him back.

'You came to intercept her,' the mortal suggested. It was a statement rather than an enquiry.

'That is so,' the king admitted.

'To try to reach agreement over the Indian boy?'

The mortal appeared to have surprising insight, but then maybe he was one of the very rare halflings with a stronger strain of fairy than mortal in their makeup. There were a few, the king had heard, though to this date he had never met one.

'You know of the boy?'

'Oh yes,' the mortal said. 'I know all about him. In a manner of speaking, you could say he is mine.'

'Your child?' This would put an altogether different complexion on the matter. 'I had thought, have been advised, that he was the son of an Indian prince.'

'Not mine in that sense,' the mortal said. 'But I invented him. So you might say he is more mine than if he were spawned by my own seed. He is rather the seed of – what shall we say? – my imagination. And now he threatens to disrupt my play. Not that that in itself matters – I am in fact rather in favour of disruptions – but with the consequent problems between your royal selves it leaves things stuck. And the groundlings simply won't stand for that.'

'I see,' said the king, who did not see at all. But at that moment the moonlight intensified and then guttered like a mighty candle.

'The queen, I suppose,' said the halfling. He moved behind his tree.

The king, left alone and caught off guard, drew himself up to his greatest height. Quite what that was would be hard to quantify but it had the effect of his seeming to tower above the queen when she swept into the glade followed by her extensive retinue. The king had wanted this advantage since he was not sanguine that his speech would carry weight. But to his surprise he found that words came to him easily.

'Ill met by moonlight, proud Titania,' he declaimed.

The queen with her teeming train of followers halted and looked up at him with long darkening eyes.

'What, jealous Oberon? Fairies, skip hence; I have forsworn his bed and company.'

The row was predictably intense and prolonged but on both sides unusually articulate. If, in the end, unproductive. The king tried one final time. To assert his claim – 'Give me that boy' – and the queen refused him yet again, 'Not for thy fairy kingdom' before commanding her followers to retire.

The king stood watching their departure until the quiet accent of the halfling in his ear made him jump. 'One of my better scenes.'

'Your scenes?'

'I wrote it.' The king stared into the patch of darkness which was the stranger's face. 'You spoke the lines superbly, that I grant you,' the easy voice continued. 'But the question is, where do we go from here?'

'Mortals alone know,' exclaimed the king, thoroughly put out. He had heard himself denounced for infidelity and then had heard his own voice in turn denouncing the queen for similar indiscretions. This sort of ugly accusation was quite unlike their usual exchanges. Vicious as each could be in turn, they had always presented blind eyes to any such irregularities.

The voice of the halfling chimed into his thoughts. 'Since you mention it, I do, as it happens, have a plan. You see, you cannot cure an obsession. You can only replace it with another one. The queen is in love with a mortal – ergo, she is, in a sense, in love with mortality. If you desire for whatever reasons that particular scrap of mortality for yourself, then you must find another mortal creature for her to dote on.'

The king, lost for words with which to meet this bizarre suggestion, said nothing.

'No doubt you will have knowledge of some

philtre drawn from the juice of a flower that will cause a body to fall in love,' the stranger went on. 'May I suggest that you ask one of your minions to fetch it for you, anoint the eyes of the queen while she is sleeping – most likely you will find her on that bank she likes to lie on for its pleasing scent of aromatic herbs – while I arrange for some suitable – or shall we say *un*suitable –' he gave a little giggle – 'mortal to appear and then *wham, bam, thank you ma'am*! as they will say in times to come when happily I shall not be around to wince at the words. I can easily work all that business into what I am planning for my drama. And, listen,' he added, 'I'll write you a scene-stopper for the moment when you determine all this. In fact, I have the opening lines already: *I know a bank where the wild thyme blows, Where oxlips and the nodding violet grows* . . . Thyme and violets bloom at quite different times of the year, I needn't tell you, but as the pair of you have fairly muddled the seasons I think I can get away with it and anyway most people know next to nothing about natural history. They won't notice, or only one or two. And those few will enjoy putting me right. I sometimes think,' the loquacious halfling continued, 'that I owe that kind, the all-knowing ones, the odd chance to set me straight. And it saves me time and bother, having to look things up to check, you know.'

He looked down at the king, who had dwindled

from the imposing lofty stature with which he had challenged the queen to a faint sliver of grey shadow. 'What do you say?'

'Will it work?'

'Of course it will work,' the halfling said. 'I will write it for you.'

The following day the king was alarmed to observe the queen, apparently in a fugue, wander past him in the woods, her arms draped dreamily about a brawny workman whose thick neck concluded in a head which seemed to be in the grotesque like-ness of an ass. The hairy temples were crowned with a garland of fresh flowers on which the dew glistened like tears. Lagging behind this ill-matched couple was a small, brown-faced boy, whose eyes, under the king's scrutiny, also looked somewhat dewy.

The king stepped in front of the boy. 'Would you like to come and live with me?'

The boy looked at him earnestly. 'Will you teach me to fly?'

The king considered. 'I don't know that I can,' he said. 'But we can always try.'

'Then I will come,' said the boy. 'Excuse me.' He ran to catch up with the queen, addressed a few words to her and then ran back to where the king stood looking after. 'She says that I may do as I like.'

'And you would like . . .?'

'If it please your majesty, to come with you. The queen is very kind but I am very, very bored.'

The flying lessons did not go well. The king made a desultory effort or two and then handed the matter over to Monkshood, who had not flown in years. After one or two dangerous falls he also passed Manu on to a minion who had no time for mortals. Manu did not fare well either as the king's henchman. He grew too large and his early aptitude for camouflage deserted him. If anything, he became something of a nuisance.

And for whatever reason, the king appeared to have lost interest in his trophy. He and the queen, whom he had released from the artfully induced passion for her asinine lover, were enjoying one of their erotic reunions and if they remembered the little Indian orphan at all it was with faint embarrassment.

One moonlit night, Manu, at a loose end and wandering alone in the woods, came to a circle of birch trees. The blades of grass were etched brightly in the light of the bold moon. Crouching to look at their delicate beauty the boy observed the figure of a man lolling against the trunk of one of the white-barked trees.

'Good evening,' the man said.

'Good evening,' Manu replied. Although he had

been brought up speaking Fairy, he had learned some human speech from listening to the children playing in the woods.

'You will be the Indian child,' the man said. 'What do they call you?'

'I am called Manu,' Manu said. This was the first mortal he had ever spoken to but he was strangely unafraid.

'I am sorry,' the man said. 'I see that I've neglected you.'

Manu frowned. 'Neglected?' It was not a word he recognised.

'I clean forgot you,' the strange man went on. 'You were a problem. In the way. Holding affairs up. I sorted you out and then you drifted out of my mind. I am sorry,' he repeated. 'One should not abandon one's creations, however much independent life one endows them with. Even the minor parts need attention.'

'I don't understand,' Manu said. He felt tearful.

The man got up. 'No, you wouldn't. I am sorry for that too. Look here, you know, you can never fly. It's not in the script.'

'I don't know what you are talking about,' Manu said. And then he did begin to cry in earnest.

'Listen,' said the man. 'You don't belong here. They're a fickle lot, fairies. They can't help it – it's their immortal nature. They wanted you in the first place because you have something they don't have:

mortality. It fascinates them because for them death is the unknown. A kind of forbidden fruit.' He squatted down beside Manu and put an arm around the boy's shoulders. Unused to the breath of mortals, Manu recoiled a little. 'Now,' said the man. 'See here. You've been raised Fairy and I've more than a dash of it in my veins. We two will get on. You come with me and I'll write you other parts.'

'Shall I be able to fly in them?' Manu asked.

'You'll be able to do any mortal thing,' the man said. 'Flying's for immortals. Mortality has more interesting things to offer. Though before you decide . . .' He put his other arm round the boy's shoulders holding him tight. In the growing light of the moon, Manu met a level green-eyed stare. 'It is midsummer now. And my mind tends towards a comic turn. But there will be winters coming and sadder tales to tell. I should warn you of this. You may also be asked to play, well, the full range. If you stay here with them, you'll grow but you'll never die.'

'They don't fly much themselves,' Manu said. 'Not at all, really.'

'There you are then,' the man said. 'My name's William, by the way. Will, if you prefer.'

They walked off together under the high yellow moon.

THE BURIED LIFE

(i)

Light flows our war of mocking words

Laura was not too surprised when Simon asked her to marry him. But she was surprised at herself when she accepted the proposal. She did not love Simon – had never pretended to, not even to herself – and so she was annoyed to find when he asked, quite ardently for him, 'How would you react to being asked to be Mrs Kraemer?' – herself answering, 'With wonder!'

Afterwards she felt it was too late to explain she had been mistaken in the impression she had given, although she was aware that this situation, whether it ended in her carrying out or reneging on the apparent promise of her words, was likely to lead to trouble.

From time to time Laura had thought about her reasons for having got in tow with Simon in the first place, and had concluded they were mainly physical. Simon was a good-looking man, tall above the average and, when she first met him, with a head of curly hair, which had since suffered the usual ravages of time, and a sensual mouth which had not. A friend of Laura's, when shown a photograph of Simon, had described the mouth as 'cruel', but Laura preferred to see in it a reference to the mouths of archaic statues, which together they visited at various ancient sites.

Laura had always known there was an element of wish-fulfilment in her observations about Simon: he was dangerous, her bones told her so, and yet, perversely, she allowed the relationship to continue, to flourish even. Her reservations had taken shape when, early in their acquaintance, she had sent Simon a poem.

It is not sensible to set tests and the poem was something of a test. Poems had become stepping-stones by which she negotiated her daily life, and this one in particular: 'The Buried Life' by Matthew Arnold.

The poem was important to her because it defined something she recognised yet had not experienced: the moment that can flash between human beings, making a home-coming of their apartness.

In general, Laura knew, life was not like that and so far had certainly not been so for her. Mostly one struggled to make oneself understood – if one struggled at all, and hadn't become accustomed to vague acquiescence in views one didn't really hold.

She had married Terence for her mother, who, as she liked to say rather often, had 'lost' her own husband and felt that a son-in-law who knew how to fix a washing machine and run down to the shops when she was out of something was just the ticket. Laura, who had spent her adolescence in rather ordinary rebellion, succumbed to the passionate love which, despite herself, she bore her mother. Finally she married Terence because she hoped this might make her mother content with her at last.

Her mother had become content, but not with Laura.

With Terence her mother had formed an alliance which included an undeclared agreement between them over Laura. 'Our girl's a bit of an idealist,' she had used to say, winking at Terence when Laura had suggested that abortion might not be the only solution for foetal abnormality. 'Wait till she has to bring up a handicapped child!'

Perhaps it was the discernible threat behind this remark which had dissuaded Laura from having the amniocentesis before giving birth to Luke, her second child. Luke, tiny, wrinkled and with one perfect arm tucked under his armpit, had been born with the other tapering into a little cleft stub. Terence had taken one look at Luke and had spoken of 'places' where the baby might be 'helped'. Laura had spent the night in terrified tears and at six the following morning had presented herself to the staff on the ward, washed and dressed with baby Luke in her arms.

'No thank you,' she had said when they suggested she wait for her husband. 'I have ordered a taxi – it is quite all right.'

Arriving home she found her mother was staying. The supper things had not been washed and a bottle of whisky was on the table. 'Celebrating, darling!' Terence had said. Later her mother found a moment to whisper, 'He was upset, you see. Dearest girl, I hope you don't mind, but a man needs a drink at times like this.'

Laura gave up her regular job as a teacher to look after Luke. Nellie, her daughter, six years older and bright as paint, helped too, and, in time, Luke learned to be almost as able as other children. But still Laura would only work in the evenings when the children were in bed, which is how, as a teacher of adult education, she met Simon.

Simon was the local organiser for adult education. 'Have you ever given your body in a sacred cause?' he asked after a few too many glasses of Chardonnay at the Christmas party. He had brown eyes which looked right into hers.

'Never!' she had replied, laughing in spite of herself and he had gravely explained that to sleep with a man on first meeting was considered by certain tribes a sign of possession by the gods. 'What a winning excuse,' she had said, still laughing and wishing that the years of maternity had left her wit in better order.

The children's annual visit to Terence's parents coinciding with the Christmas party had left Laura unusually free and she had prescribed herself the overnight stay with Simon as a restorative, hardly expecting to hear from him again. 'I'm allegedly phoning about your class on the Nineteenth-Century Novel,' he had said on the phone the following evening, 'but really it's to say "hurry back".' Terence, whose infrequent meetings with his own mother made him more than usually impatient, yelled at that moment, 'Can you get off the phone, I'm expecting someone?' which enabled Laura to say to Simon, quite properly, 'May I call you back later?' and 'Remind me of your number.'

Later she did call him and the evening classes she 'taught' began gently to expand. 'I hope they're paying you decently for all this god-awful work?' Terence had said, truculent that he had to spend yet another evening alone. 'Never mind – it'll help pay for the French trip.'

'I'll have to cut down on this,' Laura had said that evening, lying beneath Simon. Later, coming into the bedroom with a cup of coffee for her before she drove home, Simon said, 'Why not come and live with me?' and then when she said nothing, 'Marry me. I'll be fine with Luke. Look, I love your children.'

'But you haven't met them.' Laura had pointed out. Still, his offer was seductive. Far more than the call to her body, Simon's readiness to take on a handicapped boy reached to something deep inside her.

It was this exchange which, a month or so later, prompted her to send him 'The Buried Life'. By this time, Simon had taken a university job and had moved to London. She found reasons to visit him there – a conference on George Eliot, a visit to the National Gallery – but their meetings had become harder to arrange and perhaps this too was behind Laura's sending the poem.

(ii)
A Nameless Sadness

'Loved the poem!' Simon sounded breezy over the phone. A prickle across Laura's skin warned her to drop the subject, but there is a demon inside us which urges towards our own harm.

'I love it too. What did you like in it?' She was about to add, 'I couldn't send it to anyone who didn't understand.'

'I read it aloud to Trish.'

Trish was Simon's flat-mate, brought in to help pay the rent. A pale girl with black-rimmed eyes, she smiled a good deal but on the few occasions when Laura had stayed the night she had caught something baleful in Trish's glance. Sometimes she had been apprehensive lest Trish get hold of Terence's phone number.

'Oh?'

'We thought it was a bit long-winded, but then they were, weren't they, those eighteenth-century bods.'

'Matthew Arnold's nineteenth century.'

'Of course he is,' said Simon. 'Anyway, when are you coming next? My body misses yours.'

Laura had never again alluded to 'The Buried Life'. On her next visit to London she had seen the copy of the poem she had sent, which Simon and Trish had dealt with so comprehensively, lying in the dish which acted as the flat's filing system, along with the gas and electricity bills and the tokens Simon was saving from the petrol station.

That night Simon had asked again if she would come to live with him and she knew she did not want to. But it is hard, when you have established patterns, to change them. In a world of Terence, Simon was more than an escape: and he was ardent, in a way which disarmed her.

It was not until she upped sticks and brought the children to London to be with Simon that she saw a flicker in that ardour.

Simon was as good as his word – he behaved with overt kindness towards Luke, and Luke, unused to receiving the love of more than one parent, prospered. To Laura's surprise it was Nellie who was the fly in the ointment of their new life. For, gradually she became aware, the bitter truth was that Nellie and Simon did not get on.

Used to the customary daily friction between Terence and Luke, Laura was lulled at first into a false sense of the success of her enterprise when she saw the way Simon responded to her son. 'Come on, tiger,' he had said, when Luke had asked if he could 'wee' the first time they all went out together to the pictures. And he had taken Luke's hand and led him to the Gents as if the boy were his own.

Laura, in the darkness of the cinema, wept tears of gratitude. But Nellie, precocious, independent Nellie, had insisted on sitting on her lap. 'Hey, what's all this?' Laura asked. 'Nellephants don't generally sit on laps – not that I'm complaining, mind,' she added, feeling her daughter's slight frame tense. 'It's well known it's a privilege to have a Nellephant sit on one.'

'She's got an Oedipus complex,' said Simon when two nights running they had woken to find Nellie in bed with them.

Nellie, who had been taken by Laura to all kinds of theatrical events, said scornfully, 'No, I haven't – that's when a man wants to sleep with his mother. I'm not a man.'

'Perhaps you are!' Simon had replied. 'Perhaps you are going to grow a little penis and turn into a man.'

Laura had been horrified at this and Nellie had gone first red and then white and had vanished from the room.

'Simon, that was horrible.'

'It was a joke?'

'She's ten, Simon, an age where it's perfectly normal to get into your parents' bed. You might even take it as a compliment.'

But it wasn't a compliment and Laura knew she was trying to put a false complexion on things.

Luke settled down in a local school but Nellie, formerly top of her class, fell behind. She complained of stomach aches, took days off from school and became picky about her food, until Laura began to wonder if she should take her to the doctor.

'Do you think she's anorexic?' asked Simon one evening. Nellie had retreated to her room again and Simon was watching television with Luke on his knee. He sounded almost pleased with the idea.

'Don't!' Laura was at her wits' end. Her daughter's strong young body had become thin and bowed, like the body of a little old woman, and her eyes had begun to gleam unnervingly in her narrowing face. She looks like a trapped vole or a hedgehog, Laura thought, compunction twisting her heart.

Alas! is even love too weak
To unlock the heart, and let it speak?

By the time he was eleven, Luke was able to play the trumpet, football and the lead in *Richard III*, which last he did with alacrity, leaping and grinning with an energetic malevolence which belied the sweetness of his nature. Laura, now forty, sat with Simon in the school hall and felt that perhaps she had been right to leave Terence all those years ago. Terence, too, it must be said was apparently happier. He had married a former friend of Laura's who had demonstrated her friendship by working up a steady antagonism towards her husband's former wife. Laura and Simon had shaken down together; it was true that the ardour which had so forcefully won her had abated, and over the years Simon had tended to arrive home later and later from work. Laura did not enquire too deeply

173

into the possible reasons for this. It was enough for her that they were friends, of a kind, and rubbed along. And it must be owned that Simon had remained very attached to Luke. But Luke was not her only child.

Nellie, or Nell, as she was now known, bore no relation to the small eager girl who had once helped rear and care for Luke. At twelve she had started to smoke, covertly at first, later she was more brazen about it. Her room, once clinical in its neatness, became first untidy, then chaotic and finally, Laura in despair had to own, disgusting.

'Darling, how can you?' she had asked in genuine bewilderment when she had found a used tampon on her daughter's floor. And Nell had just smiled her barren little smile and shrugged and gone off with 'friends' who looked to Laura like the inmates of a detention centre.

By unspoken agreement, Laura and Simon ceased to discuss Nell. Laura, who by now held a university post, acquired the habit of racing home before Simon to tidy Nell's bedroom. Nell had placed an embargo on anyone entering her bedroom, but Laura could not bring herself to ignore the astonishing mess in which her once fastidious daughter now chose to live. Cigarette ends, used tissues, as well as other items more personal, lay littered about the room. In fact, it was through her surreptitious cleaning of Nell's room that Laura learned her daughter was no longer a virgin. She flushed the used condom down the lavatory, went downstairs and made herself a cup of coffee and smoked one of the cigarettes she had found lying in the middle of the floor.

She had not smoked for seventeen years. She found she was missing Terence.

It took a while for Laura to cotton on to the fact that Nell was taking drugs. She asked advice of a friend who had trained as a counsellor, who suggested she leave her purse lying around. 'It's a sure-fire test,' Judy had said. 'Don't leave too much in it. But if she's been honest in the past . . .'

'Of course she has!' Laura could hardly bear that she was having this conversation about her daughter. She recalled Nell at five, slipping her pocket-money into her mother's purse – not the other way round. Later, when asked why she had done this, Nellie had replied, 'To buy you nice things, 'course.'

'OK, but they change.' Judy sounded complacent. 'So if she's not taken money before and now she does, you'll know it's drugs.'

Laura, feeling like a traitor, left her purse with a twenty-pound note in it on the sideboard, on an occasion she knew Nell would be alone in the house. She spent the evening at dinner with friends, almost sweating with anxiety, and became ebullient when she found on her return that the purse had been left untouched.

'Hey, what's got into you?' Simon asked that night. 'Wild woman.'

But the short period of elation passed. It became impossible to ignore the fact that Nell, when not angry and snarling, or, somehow worse, dissociated and vague, was rendering herself comatose. It was some comfort, Laura supposed, that, at any rate, Nell showed no disposition to rob anyone in the household for her habit. A remnant of her former being, stiff and honest, still hung painfully about her and Laura sometimes thought she glimpsed a wistfulness in her daughter's eyes. But when she tried to hug her, Nell's body still seized up.

And there was no one to talk to about it. Unable to commune with Simon, Laura held back from confiding elsewhere. It was as if, were she to speak her terror, her whole life might spin out of control. She took to praying, furtively at odd moments, and to lighting candles. She threw silver coins into wishing wells, gave money to gypsies selling 'white heather' and sent sums of money, larger than she could afford, to charitable organisations – as if by virtue of the anonymity of the gift her daughter might be granted grace.

But Nell just grew less and less like the child Laura remembered. Maybe I was wrong about her? she thought. Maybe all along she was like this? But she knew she wasn't wrong. Over the years she had become shaky – her confidence in her own judgement diminished. But she clung fast to the conviction that she knew her own child.

Laura was up in Nell's room, which had become something of a fetish for her, one chilly summer evening. Simon was giving one of his 'late' seminars and Luke had gone over to a friend to spend the night. Laura, unable to resist the allure of the chaos of her daughter's room, was on her knees piling together some scattered papers when her gaze became transfixed by some words on the page before her.

Dear Daddy, she read. *Please, please trust me. I am fine. Mum, of course, as you say, is mad. She's quite barking and I have to ignore anything she tells me or I will go mad too.*

There was more but Laura did not want to read it. She walked out of her daughter's room and down the stairs and into the garden.

It was a large garden, for London, and Laura had taken pride in the way she had planted it. A tree, a shrub, a scented plant, a herb for every birthday, every anniversary – every important family occasion. She went and lay face down now under the white lilac tree she had planted for the third anniversary of her meeting with Simon.

'Nellie, Nellie.' She found she was crying and scratching the ground. Earth was in her mouth and the damp grass was soaking her clothes. 'Nellie,

Nellie, Nellie – my little Nellephant – What have I done to you? Oh, Nellie!' For it was she, she – she couldn't any longer avoid the frightful knowledge – she who had done this to her own child.

She had left Terence so that Luke might have a chance – and in doing so had destroyed her daughter. No. That was a lie. She had left Terence for her own selfish interests – because, frankly, she could no longer bear – had loathed, in fact, his way of pulling down all that seemed good to her. But she had had children by Terence. By the inescapable law of nature she was not entitled to leave. And for what had she left, after all? Rolling over on to her back she thought about Simon.

She had known all there was to know about her and Simon from the beginning: the poem she had sent had told her. Simon had no clue what 'The Buried Life' might mean. And she had gone on, knowing he had no clue, forcing her child into a picture of a life which suited herself for the time being. And in return for this her child had turned on her – and who could blame her? 'Oh, Nellie, Nellie,' she cried, and from the cold grass and white London skies no answer came to give her comfort.

(iv)

And long we try in vain to speak and act
Our hidden self, and what we say and do
Is eloquent, is well – but 'tis not true!

Some vestige of strength, some particle of the years of early care, must have remained in Nell, for she got herself into university. Simon was delighted; he even offered to help her transport her things. Laura could not banish the notion that his enthusiasm was fuelled by his desire to see Nell out of their house. 'D'you think she's ready for it?' Laura asked him, as they prepared for bed the night before Nell's departure.

'Sure. She'll have a whale of a time. Do her good. Get her away from her mama's beady eye. You'll see – it'll be cool!'

But Laura, who tried not to object to the over-youthful turns of speech that Simon increasingly tended to use, remained uneasy. Nell had displayed uncharacteristic signs of nerves about her impending experience.

'C'm on! That's normal,' Simon had said. 'Give the girl a break!' And the following morning, when Nell was looking green over her breakfast coffee: 'What about a nip of whisky for the university girl? Get you into the student mood.'

With Nell gone, the household, it was true, grew calmer. The effort which had gone into Luke's care had brought compensations. He was popular, and there were few weekends Laura and Simon did not now have to themselves. Laura felt guilty to find that life without Nell was pleasanter. And of course, much of the relief came from the effect her daughter's departure had on Simon.

'It's great to be alone together again,' he said one night in the bath. And as she climbed out of her clothes to join him, 'This is like old times.'

So when Simon asked Laura to marry him she was not much surprised, only at the form she found her answer taking.

'I always said we should marry,' said Simon. 'D'you remember? Thirteen years and I've never wanted another woman.'

Perhaps by an association of ideas (she was thinking of his 'late' seminars) Laura found herself asking, 'Whatever happened to Trish?' The flat-mate with the baleful eye had caused some trouble when asked to make way for Laura's children. But the departed Trish had continued to send Simon a Christmas card each year, until one year they had stopped.

Simon flushed suddenly and looked angry. 'Why d'you want to know about her all of a sudden?'

'Just wondered,' said Laura lightly. She was amused, and for some reason rather relieved, that her intuitions about Simon were accurate.

Although it is surely barmy to be feeling this over a man you are about to marry, she said to herself later as, Simon downstairs watching TV, she settled down in bed to read.

Laura and Simon were to spend their honeymoon in Greece. It was a country they had visited often, a place where they had had happy times. Simon was at his best talking about the anthropology of ancient cultures and Laura liked the bareness of the landscape and the ancient sites.

It was at Epidaurus, staying in a modest little hotel, that the call came. A knocking at the bedroom door and Laura, summoned from sleep, found the proprietor outside.

'Forgive,' he said, twisting his hands. 'I do not wish to wake you but there is a telephone.' He gestured down the dimly lighted stairs.

'For me, or my husband?' asked Laura, also making explanatory gestures.

'For lady called Ken – er, please?'

Kennedy was Terence's name. 'What is it, darling?' Simon called from the bed.

'It's OK – it's for me, I think – he wants me to go to the phone downstairs.'

'Oh, Christ! Get him to put it through.'

'Please?' said the fat proprietor, gesturing again.

'No, look, it's easier if I go with him.'

She knew already who it would be.

'Mum?'

'Nell? Whatever time of night is it?'

'Sorry. Did I get you up?'

'Nell, what time is it? Where are you calling from?'

'Dunno the time – 'bout one o'clockish?'

'What's happened? Are you OK?' But of course she wasn't. Nell of all people would not phone unless she was in trouble. Big trouble.

'Look, don't get excited, but it's the police.'

'What?'

'I'm in a police station.'

'Oh, Nell!' Nellie, my little girl, my Nellie. 'Darling, what's happened?'

'They let me call you.'

And Nell had had the number. Laura put away for later contemplation the knowledge that her daughter had kept about her the means of finding her mother. 'Darling, shall I call you back?'

'No,' said Nell. 'You might not get through. I'm scared I mightn't get you again.'

(v)

As from an infinitely distant land,
Come airs, and floating echoes, and convey
A melancholy into all our day

It was getting light when she returned to the bedroom. Simon was snoring and she had to shake him.

'What's up?'

'Terence, I have to go home.'

Simon sat up in bed rubbing his forehead. 'You called me Terence!'

'Sorry. I'm a bit frantic.'

'Jesus Christ, Laura, you called me Terence!'

'I'm sorry. It's Nell.' The blue Greek bedspread was an ocean between them in the hardening light. I hate you, she thought. I actually hate you, God forgive me!

'Of course it's Nell.' As if reading her thoughts his voice had taken on a hateful sneer. 'Ickle Nellsie-wellsie calling her mumsy-wumsy home.'

183

Laura stared at him. His face looked peevish and infantile. Men are like wine: the best mature, the rest turn to vinegar. Who was it said that?

'Nevertheless, I'm afraid I have to go.' There was something in the 'Nevertheless' which gave her courage. 'She's been detained by the police on drugs charges. Her father is out of the country and there's no one to help her. I'm afraid I must go back.'

'You're out of the country too! In fact, you're out of your fucking mind.' There was nothing to say to a man who needed such a thing explained to him. Her daughter, in trouble, had called on her; it was as simple as that. She stood there, looking at him, noting the receding hairline with a kind of satisfaction. 'Well, you'll have to go without me, I'm afraid.'

Poor Simon. His veiled threat was pathetic. She didn't really hate him. 'I know that.'

Downstairs, the proprietor's wife gave her bitter coffee and a dry-as-dust roll. The woman placed a bowl of honey carefully on the table, as if to communicate her awareness of a trouble fallen on her guest. 'Excuse me – a car – could you tell me how to hire a car?' The car they had hired was in Simon's name.

The woman looked concerned. 'Here was cars but now . . .' She shrugged, indicating some incommunicable local calamity. 'No cars.'

'But the nearest one? I need to get to Athens urgently.' She nearly said, It's my daughter. The

184

woman gave every sign that she would understand.

The proprietor's wife said something in Greek and then went and fetched her husband with the black and mournful moustache.

'There is no car here for hire, but if it is an emergency I give you the number of Mr Acton. He is an English gentleman, very nice. He live up there.' He pointed to a stone house set back a little way up the hillside.

An Englishman. Well he would understand her need at least. He might help her get to Athens.

'Would he mind if I called?'

The proprietor nodded as if he was in the habit of setting his more problematic guests off on Mr Acton.

Hurrying along the road, Laura wondered what she was going to say. The door of the house had the appearance of being locked and she had to steel herself to bang loudly. But there was Nell waiting for her, in a cell in Camden Town.

'Forgive me. You don't know me from Adam. I'm Laura Kennedy.'

He was a big man with a shabby-looking face and bedroom slippers. 'You need help?'

She nearly kissed his hand. 'I need to get to Athens urgently.'

'And there is no car. So, is it a particular flight you need?'

'Any flight to London – but as soon as possible.'

The man indicated she should come inside and she entered, behind him, into a stone-flagged room. He picked up a phone and spoke into it in Greek.

Finishing the conversation, he said, 'There are no cars to hire here at present but mine will be available in thirty minutes. It will take six to eight hours to reach Athens, which means you may catch today's three o'clock flight to Heathrow. I cannot promise, but I will do my best.'

'Is it the only flight? I'm sorry, that sounds churlish . . .'

She was shaking and perhaps observing this he said, 'Won't you sit down? I'm afraid it's the last, until the following morning, that is. Please, sit. Unless you have baggage to fetch . . .?'

That would mean seeing Simon again. She had her bag, her passport. 'I have all I need.'

'That's good,' said the man calmly. He had the slight old-fashioned tinge to his English which comes from living many years abroad. 'May I offer you coffee? Some ouzo?'

'Coffee would be marvellous.'

He moved about the kitchen filling a kettle. His movements, Laura noticed, were slow. 'Excuse my discourtesy – I have failed to introduce myself. I am Matthew Acton – Matt to my friends. I have lived here thirty years.'

'The travel writer?' She had heard of him.

'Indeed. Although nowadays I don't travel so much. These days I spin yarns.'

'About the travel?'

'About whatever comes to mind. I sell old memories – or rather my agent sells them for me. It keeps body and soul together and life here is, or has been, anyway, still fairly cheap.'

She sensed he was deliberately keeping from anything which might seem like an enquiry. 'Look, I'm so grateful . . .'

'Please.' He looked at her and she saw something.

'Your eyes,' she cried. His eyes were of quite different colours, one blue, one brown.

'Yes. My mother, who was foremost among yarn-spinners, claimed it was because I was conceived under a hazel-bush. She liked to pretend it bestowed occult powers. A good ploy, I found, for getting girls into bed. Here, would you like brandy in it?'

'Please.' He poured a large measure into the green cup. Sipping it and feeling the hot coffee and alcohol begin to warm her, she said, 'My daughter's being held by the police. That's why I have to get to London.'

'Naturally. Don't worry, I'm a fast driver.'

Somehow she hadn't taken in that he proposed driving her himself. 'Oh, but isn't that an awful nuisance?'

'What is more important – the nuisance you cause me or your debt to your daughter?'

Debt. It was a funny word to choose. 'Do you have children?' she asked.

'None I've been introduced to.'

'I have two,' she said. 'A daughter and a son.'

'So?' he said. 'Two. I envy you. Listen, that noise like a Jabberwock you hear is Michaelis returning my car!'

(vi)
Only – but this is rare –

It was ten past two when they reached Athens Airport.

Laura, before she left the car, said, 'I'll never be able to thank you.'

'Then don't try – I've enjoyed it. I've already turned it, in my head, into a yarn. Beautiful damsel in distress at my door at dawn.'

'Hardly a damsel!'

'Still beautiful though.' One blue-grey eye, one conker-brown looked at her. 'Married?' In six hours he hadn't asked a single personal question.

Relentless Time was speeding past. 'I was here on my honeymoon. Look, would you write your address for me?'

'Here,' he said, and she noticed, taking the scrap of paper from his hand, he was still wearing his slippers. 'If you hurry you will be with your daughter by this evening. One night in the cells will be no more than a yarn for her to dine out on later. She might be able to spin it into gold, you never know.'

'A yarn?' There was no time to explain about Simon.

'You can't start too early with yarns.'

After she had bought the ticket she went back out to the forecourt to see if he were still there, but he had gone. So she was unable to tell him he shared a first name – indeed the initials – of her favourite poet.

And what we mean, we say . . .

Dear Matthew Acton,
     Thank you so much. The enclosed is a copy
of my favourite poem.
     Yours,
     Laura Kennedy

The Buried Life
Light flows our war of mocking words, and yet,
Behold, with tears mine eyes are wet!
I feel a nameless sadness o'er me roll.
Yes, yes, we know that we can jest,
We know, we know that we can smile!
But there's a something in this breast,
To which thy light words bring no rest,
And thy gay smiles no anodyne;
Give me thy hand, and hush awhile,

And turn those limpid eyes on mine,
And let me read there, love! thy inmost soul.

Alas! is even love too weak
To unlock the heart, and let it speak?
Are even lovers powerless to reveal
To one another what indeed they feel?
I knew the mass of men conceal'd
Their thoughts, for fear that if reveal'd
They would by other men be met
With blank indifference, or with blame reprov'd;
I knew they liv'd and mov'd
Trick'd in disguises, alien to the rest
Of men, and alien to themselves – and yet
The same heart beats in every human breast!

But we, my love! – doth a like spell benumb
Our hearts, our voices? – must we too be dumb?

Ah, well for us, if even we,
Even for a moment, can get free
Our heart, and have our lips unchain'd;
For that which seals them hath been deep-
    ordain'd!

Fate, which foresaw
How frivolous a baby man would be –
By what distractions he would be possess'd,
How he would pour himself in every strife,

And well-nigh change his own identity –
That it might keep from his capricious play
His genuine self, and force him to obey
Even in his own despite his being's law,
Bade through the deep recesses of our breast
The unregarded river of our life
Pursue with indiscernible flow its way;
And that we should not see
The buried stream, and seem to be
Eddying at large in blind uncertainty,
Though driving on with it eternally.

But often, in the world's most crowded streets,
But often, in the din of strife,
There rises an unspeakable desire
After the knowledge of our buried life;
A thirst to spend our fire and restless force
In tracking out our true, original course;
A longing to enquire
Into the mystery of this heart which beats
So wild, so deep in us – to know
Whence our lives come and where they go.

And many a man in his own breast then delves,
But deep enough, alas! none ever mines.
And we have been on many, thousand lines.
And we have shown, on each, spirit and power;
But hardly have we, for one little hour,
Been on our own line, have we been ourselves

Hardly had skill to utter one of all
The nameless feelings that course through our
   breast,
But they course on for ever unexpress'd.
And long we try in vain to speak and act
Our hidden self, and what we say and do
Is eloquent, is well – but 'tis not true!
And then we will no more be rack'd
With inward striving, and demand
Of all the thousand nothings of the hour
Their stupefying power;
Ah yes, and they benumb us at our call!
Yet still, from time to time, vague and forlorn,
From the soul's subterranean depth upborne
As from an infinitely distant land,
Come airs, and floating echoes, and convey
A melancholy into all our day.

Only – but this is rare –
When a beloved hand is laid in ours,
When, jaded with the rush and glare
Of the interminable hours,
Our eyes can in another's eyes read clear,
When our world-deafen'd ear
Is by the tones of a lov'd voice caress'd –
A bolt is shot back somewhere in our breast,
And a lost pulse of feeling stirs again.
The eye sinks inward, and the heart lies plain,

And what we mean, we say, and what we would,
  we know.
A man becomes aware of his life's flow,
And hears its winding murmur; and he sees
The meadows where it glides, the sun, the
  breeze.

And there arrives a lull in the hot race
Wherein he doth forever chase
The flying and elusive shadow, rest.
An air of coolness plays upon his face,
And an unwonted calm pervades his breast.
And then he thinks he knows
The hills where his life rose,
And the sea where it goes.

Matthew Arnold

MOVING

They had been packing for hours. Cardboard boxes, bandaged with brown sticky tape and marked with cryptic messages as to their content, stood as a bulwark against chaos among the litter of tin openers, screwdrivers, weather-blackened clothes pegs, dish cloths, unravelled hanks of garden twine, a nest of withered daffodil bulbs and the singular cherubic head of a doll which looked hard at no one with dead blue eyes.

Beneath the head with its dainty rosebud lips, Jacob, as if avoiding the remorseless blue stare, lay on a floor bare of its Turkish rugs upon a stack of folded blankets destined for any charity shop that would unbend enough to accept them. The local Oxfam shop, they had discovered, had been transformed into a chic designer emporium. What, Selina wondered, would happen now to all the bits and bobs and sharp bits, as her godmother would have called them, that until lately had so usefully been passed on for further use. The need to do good, she thought, also required some cherishing. Nowadays, charity required of its aspirants standards which they were increasingly likely to fail.

Selina looked at her friend. His body stretched out upon the stack of blankets was a medieval knight or princeling's, made marmoreal for eternity on his own tomb. 'You look like something Damien Hirst might pickle in formaldehyde,' she said, guessing that this comparison would please him more.

'I wish he would.' Jacob couldn't see Selina, who was sitting with her back straight against the wall, but he could smell that she was smoking. He wished she wouldn't. But she would know quite well what he was feeling and was presumably overriding politeness. And the house by tomorrow lunchtime would no longer be his, so what did it matter if it stank of smoke?

Aware of what was passing through her friend's mind, Selina pushed herself up, groaning a little at the stiffness, and went out into the small enclosed garden. A passionflower of deepest purple, its dark stamens forming the cross which gave it its name, was swinging one of its fronds over the lime-washed garden wall. Flowers didn't have to bother about feeling intrusive, she thought. She had helped Jacob paint that wall. This little house of peace and charm was perhaps the only place in the world where she did not feel like an intruder on God's earth, and tomorrow it would be gone. Or gone, at least, for her.

She would no longer have the use of the white upper room, full of weather because years ago the blinds had stuck and Jacob had never fixed them. When he had once tried, she had said, 'No, you can leave it. I like to see the light break.' His discretion was such that he had not made the obvious connection aloud: that she was so often awake long before dawn that to see the sun rise at last was a comfort and a release, a sign that she would not have to remain alone much longer in the dark.

'Of course,' Selina said over her shoulder from her post in the garden, 'when they come for all this tomorrow I might simply stay.'

'What do you mean?' There was a slight hint of anxiety beneath the casualness.

'I might just stay here and when the "purchaser" arrives I'll say, "You can't come in because you see I live here, so buzz off!"'

She knew that he knew that this bit of foolery on her part was not wholly impossible and he showed that he was aware of this by taking it humorously.

'Good plan. Then you could smuggle me back in and we could have our cake and eat it. Though

I never quite get what that means. Who wants to keep cake? It would grow mouldy.' No need to add that he needed the money. Neither of them wanted him to have sold.

Thinking this, she said to reassure him, 'I could stay and help you to see all this into the van tomorrow, if you wanted me to?' It would delay her return to the dim flat in Clapham, made available to her by a not so close friend while she found a more permanent place to stay.

'It's all right, I can manage.'

Selina said, 'I just wanted you to know it's on offer.' Tomorrow she would have to think of something else to do.

'If you want to, of course . . .' Jacob said. From his position on the blanket, he had caught a glimpse of her neck. Her neck, once a column of smoothness had, he saw, folds in it. The small gold and silver pendant that she always wore looked more than ever like a charm against a dangerous world. She's getting old, he thought. 'It goes without saying I'd rather you stayed.'

Selina, recognising that this was affection for her rather than any need for himself, said, 'I shall miss all this terribly.'

'Me, too.'

'Terribly,' she repeated. And then, 'Shall I open the champagne?'

'Why not?'

She had bought champagne, spending more than she could afford. The truth was she didn't much like it. But Jacob did. And she wanted them to leave the house in the spirit in which they had lived there. Was it true that there had never been a cross word between them or was that sheer sentimentality? There must have been cross thoughts but she honestly couldn't recall any. A scrap of jealousy at times, but never for his male friends. She supposed she wanted to be best for him, at least as far as women went. But that was a pipe dream. Only for babies were you ever truly number one. But she mustn't think of babies. 'Too late' her breastbone screamed.

She had taken the foil from around the cork and was untwisting the little wire cage. 'Do you want to open it?'

'No, you do it.'

She came and stood over him and the cork exploded like a fairground gun and the pale froth anointed his forehead and newly greying hair. 'I name this ship Jacob. God bless her, and all who sail in her.'

'Here,' he said, unfolding himself and holding out the couple of glasses they had spared from the packing. Not any old glasses. Long crystal glasses she had given him for no special reason. It was a rule between them that they never did Christmas or birthdays; both agreeing that the sense of require-ment ruined the pleasure in buying the gift.

They polished off the bottle before they set about the last of the packing. It was past midnight before they stopped and looked at each other, disarranged and dirty but for all the sadness of the enterprise pleased at their efficiency.

'I bet I look a fright,' Selina said.

'You always look good.'

'I wish that were true.' It had been true. Once she had almost always looked good enough.

Jacob said, 'I wish there were more champagne.'

'We could go out looking.' She hoped that they might climb into his environmentally incorrect Mercedes and trawl off into the night on a forage.

'I think I'm too weary.'

Selina said, '*I am aweary aweary, I would that I were dead . . .*'

'I hope that's not true, S.'

'Not altogether,' she said, as convincingly as she could, and kissed his cheek. He always smelled so nice. What a shame that the people you were easiest with were the people you didn't have sex with. But sex, so wonderful, so terrible, so utterly precarious, brought children.

She slept fitfully and woke the following morning long before dawn. By the time Jacob appeared downstairs she had drunk four cups of coffee and smoked three cigarettes. 'Ready, then?' She smiled dishonestly, trying to convey cheer.

'As ready as I'll ever be.'

And when the van with three men arrived, one short, stocky and young, one emaciated and old, and one nonentity, whose role seemed to be to boss the other two shockingly about, it went far easier than either of them had dreamed. In two hours, the house was empty of everything but the doll's head.

'What shall we do with this?' Jacob tossed the rubber sphere in the air and caught it with his other hand. The van had driven off and the two of them were alone again.

'When do you need to get to the storage place?' Most of his things were to go to his lover Douglas's house. But the remainder was to go into store.

'Douglas is seeing to all that.'

Selina said, 'It's Hetty's doll. She must have left the head here when you and she were playing executioners.' In the days before she lived there. In the days when she lived. When she and Hetty had their little council flat.

'Oh God.' His eyes were dark dismay. 'I'm sorry. I didn't think.'

'Why should you?'

'Let's take it to her,' Jacob said suddenly, 'or, I mean, if you wanted to . . .'

But she seemed pleased at the thought after all. 'If you wanted to . . .?'

Hester Emily Palliser's grave lay at one of the outer edges of Putney Cemetery under the shadow of a lime tree whose beneficent branches had strayed over to shade the heedless dead. The small grey slab of uncut stone merely gave her name, and the dates of her coming into the world and her swift departure. Side by side they stood contemplating this account of Selina's daughter's life – b. 10 x 2004 d. 3 iv 2007. Selina bent and laid by the stone the doll's head, which stared up at them with its blank speedwell eyes. She had planted a rose on her daughter's grave. A crop of loose, pale pink blooms exhaled a faint scent of apples in the warm air.

'What rose is it?' Jacob asked.

'A sport of the wild rose.' She had planted a root of rosemary too, but it had perished. Rosemary for remembrance. But there was no need for reminders to remember Hetty.

She had put her daughter to bed, one cool April night, kissed her and left her with her musical bell playing an old lullaby. And in the morning Hetty was dead – dead as a door nail. The investigations had been lengthy, gruelling and finally inconclusive. She knew that for ever now she would be marked down as the possible murderer of her beloved child. She didn't care. She had wished they had sent her to prison where at least her surroundings would have matched her state of heart. That she lived on at all while Hetty had gone was a cruel joke. Only some kind of sense that she ought to continue to live for the sake of her dead child – and she could not have explained or defended that decision had she been asked to – had kept her alive. That and the sanctuary of Jacob's white room in his kind house, which had housed her and her misery. Now that was gone too where on God's earth was her grief to be housed?

A single magpie flew past and settled on a nearby tomb. A tomb replete with waxen flowers in dirty glass domes. One for sorrow.

Selina picked up the doll's head. 'It looks wrong here. Would you keep it for me?'

'But don't you . . .?'

'No. I'd rather you did. She loved playing with you.'

Taking the empty head from her hand, Jacob touched her arm and said, 'We, I, I mean, should have brought her flowers. I'm sorry.'

'It doesn't matter.'

Nothing mattered any more. One day she would move for good. Until then, she must find other accommodation.

THE DEAL

'No,' Alice's mother Rosemary Armitage said, more sternly than she had perhaps intended. 'You can't have a cat. I'm sorry, but you know why. Daddy is allergic.'

'Oh *please*.'

'Love, we've been through this.'

Alice sighed. She was six years old and an only child.

'*Please*, *please*,' she said again, knowing no other way but emphasis to convey her extreme need. 'I'll keep her in the shed so Daddy won't sneeze.'

'You can't keep a cat in the shed, love. A guinea pig or a rabbit, maybe.'

But Alice didn't want a guinea pig. She wanted a marmalade cat with a white bib. A girl cat.

'Girl marmalades are very rare, sweetheart,' her father said.

His wife stared at him and baffled he returned the look. What had he said now, for God's sake?

Later, when she had got him into the kitchen his wife explained. 'George, if we don't want her to have a cat suggesting that females are hard to come by simply gives out a message that if we do find one she can have it.'

Her husband shook his head, confounded by this – perfectly sensible, if only he would think straight, Rosemary irritably said – piece of feminine reasoning.

The remark, as her mother feared, had sunk in. Alice, sitting before the TV watching her DVD of *The Sleeping Beauty*, determined that she would find a girl marmalade kitten herself. 'To hell with them!' she thought. She had heard this expression used by Mr Job, who had an allotment next to her mother's, and had been storing it up since for use at a suitable moment.

Rosemary Armitage was pleasantly surprised that her daughter had agreed so readily to accompany her to the allotment the following Sunday. As a rule, this took much cajoling if not outright bribery. Alice didn't like the muddy earth which got on her shoes or boots. It was not her opinion that boots were for getting dirty, whatever her mother said. And most decidedly she was not, as Rosemary

Armitage was, 'into' vegetables. And yet she was quite agreeable when her mother, summoning her patience for a fight, suggested that they go to dig the allotment.

Alice had a plan. She intended to sound out Mr Job and if possible recruit him in the cause of the marmalade kitten. He had shown an admirable sense of equality towards her over his use of language and general demeanour, which was that of a large and sympathetic, if slightly unpredictable, child. And luck was on her side. As they arrived at the allotment, they met Mr Job carrying a large, leaking metal watering can.

'Turning out a nice evening again, Mrs Hermitage.' Mr Job was a little deaf. Or maybe it was that he was a little mischievous. In any case he never quite seemed to manage Rosemary Armitage's name. 'Hello, Alice.' He had no trouble with hers. 'Going to pick those runner beans?'

Alice had no thoughts of helping with the beans. She made a half-hearted attempt at collecting a few of the lower ones and then sidled over to Mr Job, who was picking off the tops of his tomatoes. 'See the little 'uns here? We have to squeeze them off so these others below grow nice and fat. Want one?'

Alice, who drove her mother to distraction by dismissing tomatoes along with most other vegetables as 'yukky', sank her teeth into a large firm yellow-and-red-skinned tomato and pronounced it 'delicious'. This not entirely truthful response was made in the service of the marmalade kitten. Alice had not yet heard of the French Protestant king who felt that Paris was worth a Mass but she shared his essential pragmatism.

'They've come on grand, that strain of toms this summer,' Mr Job said, collegiately. His tone and manner decided Alice.

'Mr Job,' she said, discreetly wiping some stray tomato pips from the sleeve of her pink-glitter mermaid T-shirt. 'I need a marmalade kitten. A girl kitten,' she added with emphasis, lest there be any mistake.

'A girl ginger? They're not so thick on the ground.'

'I just need one,' Alice said, with perfect simplicity.

'Your mum say you can have it?' Mr Job was not unshrewd. For all that he liked to tease Rosemary over her name, he had nothing against her. And he had heard the arguments with Alice over the kitten.

Alice made a split-second decision and set off across the causeway which we must all pass over and which, once crossed, permits no return. 'She says I can keep it in the shed.'

'Oh well. Guess it won't know the difference. Tell you what. I'll get you a kitten for a bottle of Newcastle Brown. That's my poison. Is that a deal?'

'It's a deal,' Alice said, pleased with her newfound powers of negotiation.

Alice was preoccupied on their way home. She answered her mother abstractedly, in a manner which made Rosemary Armitage inwardly pray that the child was not going to take after her father. That night after her bath Alice asked, casually, 'What is Newscastle Brown?'

'Newcastle,' her father corrected, just as her mother asked, 'Why do you need to know that?'

'It was on TV,' Alice said.

'It's a kind of beer, love,' her mother said. 'Not a very nice one.'

'Do you have some?'

'Why?' asked her mother again, as her father was saying, 'No we don't. Revolting stuff.'

'They said on TV you could use the bottle to make a model,' Alice said, thereby answering her mother and taking a further stride away from the paradise of unquestioning childhood truthfulness.

'That's life,' she said later to her doll, Fancy Pansy. This was another expression she had been saving up. 'People believe in stupid models from TV more than in kittens.'

Rosemary was delighted at the way Alice had become so devoted to the allotment. Not that she ever did much when they got there, but, as Rosemary explained to George, the fresh air did her good and it couldn't be bad for her faddiness to be among vegetables. Much of Alice's time at the allotments, it was true, seemed to be spent with Mr Job. But he was a harmless old man, if rather deaf, though oddly he seemed to have no trouble hearing Alice. It was probably a matter of the pitch of the voice and it was nice to see their child befriending an old man.

'What if I can't get Newscastle Brown?' Alice was enquiring of Mr Job as her mother was enjoying these reassuring thoughts.

'Then no deal,' Mr Job said. 'No wriggling. Fair's fair.'

This posed a problem. Grown ups drank beer so it was especially annoying of her parents that they did not drink Mr Job's poison.

'Why is it called "poison"?' she had asked on one of the allotment visits. 'Poison's what kills people.' She knew this for sure from *The Sleeping Beauty*.

'Kind of joke,' Mr Job said briefly. He was tying up his tomatoes. 'Mind, plenty I've known's killed themselves with drink. Not Newcastle Brown, though. That is the elixir of life.'

Alice was relieved to hear this. She was fond of Mr Job, even without his kitten-providing facilities, and did not want to be the cause of his death. She had been considering at length where she might go to find a bottle of this fabulous elixir that was so precious it was the price of a marmalade kitten.

Maybe, it crossed her mind, it was just too expensive for her parents.

After some mulling, Alice settled on her father's younger brother, Steve, as the most likely source of Mr Job's poison. They were due to visit Steve in London, where he lived in a flat which was exactly the kind of place Alice was going to live in when she was older. It was extremely tidy and the toilet seat was a special see-through plastic, with shells and starfish stuck around inside, and the carpet in the bathroom had little green fishes swimming all over it and seaweed. They just had tiles on the floor at her house, which were freezing on your feet if you got out of the bath and missed the bath mat, and Daddy said that he didn't want to sit on a toilet seat with crabs in it, they might pinch his bottom, which was extremely silly of him as there were no crabs and anyway you could see they weren't live.

Uncle Steve lived with his girlfriend, Lulu, who was a dancer and standing up could put her leg behind her ear. Lulu wore perfect clothes and let Alice dress up in them and use her makeup. And best of all on these visits, she was usually left with Steve and Lulu to babysit while her parents went out for some time alone. So the chances of finding Newscastle Brown were fairly high.

'Don't worry, Mummy, I'll be fine,' Alice said. She knew her mother needed reassurance and it was easy to give since she wanted her out of the way.

'Of course she will,' her father said. 'Come on or we'll miss the start of the film. Night, sweetheart. Don't give your uncle and aunty a hard time.'

'She's not my aunty,' Alice said. On another occasion, she might have added, 'They are not married,' as this was a controversial point between her and Steve for which she had more than once had to take him to task. But for the sake of the quest for Mr Job's poison she was prepared to be indulgent.

Alice had a bath with plenty of Lulu's 'Pink Champagne' bath foam. She dried the suds from her pink limbs inside Lulu's pink towelling dressing gown and wore Lulu's mauve and silver high-heeled mules. Then she went and wedged herself between Steve and Lulu – to stop any silly stuff – on the sofa and watched her favourite London DVD which was *Bambi*. Lulu liked *Bambi* too because it made her cry.

After it was over, Steve said, 'Well, monkey, bed for you, I suppose.'

'Steve, do you have Newscastle Brown in your house?'

'What castle?'

'I *said*, Newscastle Brown.'

'That's a kind of beer. What do you want with beer, monkey?'

'Oh, this sand that,' Alice said. This phrase had also been awaiting use.

'I don't have any, I'm afraid. Now bed for you, or I'll be in trouble with your mum and dad.'

'They won't know,' Alice said. 'They're out and I shan't tell.'

'What you want my tipple for, pet?' Lulu asked. She was from Newcastle herself.

'It's Mr Job's poison,' Alice explained. 'And if I get him a bottle he'll get me a marmalade kitten. It's a deal.' It was a perfectly clear arrangement. She looked at her uncle and Lulu with eyes ready to pass an unfavourable judgement.

Luckily, her uncle was a rational sort. 'I don't have any in, as it happens,' he apologised. 'But if it's a deal, I daresay some could be found.'

'Good,' Alice said. 'I knew I could rely on you.'

Having found a use for almost all her new phrases, she went off to bed, quite contentedly, in Lulu's mules.

Getting the bottle of Newscastle Brown home was tricky but Alice managed it by wrapping it in her Dora Explorer vest and sticking it at the very bottom of her Hello Kitty backpack. Now all she had to do was be sure to unpack her backpack herself and then get the bottle to Mr Job. The first task was easy enough, since her mother was keen on her doing things for herself. The second took some planning but, as heroes often find, she was helped along by fortune.

'Alice, love, would you mind carrying the bag

with the new trowel in it? I've got to carry these steps for the beans,' her mother said when the following weekend they were preparing to go to the allotment.

'Yes, Mummy,' Alice said. 'I am glad to help.'

Her father shot her a glance. 'You all right, sweetheart?'

'Yes, Daddy,' Alice said. 'I am very well, thank you.'

She sped upstairs, removed the bottle from deep in her toy box and slipped it into the bag with the trowel.

Mr Job had apparently been waiting for her. 'I got the kitten,' he said, sounding for him almost excited. 'Ginger girl, like you ordered. Be six weeks old, near enough. So in another two she'll be yours.'

'And I,' said Alice, 'have got you your Newscastle Brown.' With a proud flourish, she presented him with the bottle wrapped in an old copy of *Princess* magazine.

'Lordy,' said Mr Job. 'I never meant you to take me seriously. How'd you get your hands on this?'

'We had a deal,' Alice said, primly. 'You said "no wriggling".' She looked reproachfully at Mr Job.

'You know what, you're a princess, you are.'

'I am going to be,' Alice agreed. 'But I have to marry a handsome prince first.'

The next step was breaking the news at home.

'Daddy,' she said, when her mother was out at

a neighbourhood meeting. 'You know how it is very, *very* hard to find a girl marmalade kitten.'

'What?' said her father, who was watching the news, which was far from reassuring.

'A girl marmalade. You said it was very, *very* hard to find one.'

''Fraid so, old girl,' said her father, absentmindedly using for his daughter the title with which he habitually annoyed his wife.

'Well, I have been very clever and found one.'

'Well done, old girl,' said her father, with his mind on the spiralling inflation.

'So I can have her, then?'

'I expect so. You'll have to ask your mother.'

Alice sighed. So near and yet so far.

She postponed tackling her mother till they were back at the allotment, perhaps because the presence of her ally Mr Job provided moral support. He grinned at them when they arrived, which for him was most unusual. Rosemary Armitage hoped that it wasn't that he was drunk.

'Evening, ladies.'

'Good evening, Mr Job. Say good evening to Mr Job, Alice.'

Alice went over to kiss Mr Job. 'Mr Job's my friend,' she announced. 'Mr Job has –' here she had to dig a little into her courage '– found me a marmalade kitten. A girl kitten. Like I wanted.' She risked a bright smile at her mother.

Rosemary Armitage's naturally anxious forehead wrinkled some more.

'Alice, love, we've had this conversation. I'm so sorry, Mr Job, but you see my husband is allergic. Alice doesn't really . . .'

'Excuse me.' Apparently ignoring Alice's beseeching look Mr Job was holding up a big, cracked, earth-impregnated hand. 'We had a deal, me and your daughter, Mrs, herahm, Armitage. See, I've had my arthritis come on badly and I might have to give up the allotment. But your daughter here has kindly said she'll help me out with the weeding. Now, that's unusual in a young girl. Kind and thoughtful she's been brought up, I can see that, Mrs, ahm, your doing I can tell. But it's only right she should have something in return. Otherwise,' his hand waved imperiously at Rosemary as she tried to break in, '*otherwise* if I don't keep my word she might get to think words can be broken and helping other people out's not worth much, if you know what I mean. Do you know what I mean?' He was smiling again – 'almost leering', Rosemary was later to describe it to her husband – showing a hideous row of broken, tobacco-stained teeth. An eavesdropper might have fancied they detected a faint menace in his tone.

'Yes,' said Rosemary Armitage, crumpling her forehead further. 'Perhaps.'

'There's injections you can have for allergies now,' continued Mr Job, confidingly. 'My sister who was allergic had them. Total success. Total success, Mrs, ahm, well.'

'Well,' said Rosemary. 'Maybe. We'll have to see.' She turned aside to move towards her beans but Mr Job stepped in front of her, almost barring her way.

'See, we had a deal, me and Alice. And I don't know if I'll be able to manage this allotment without I get some help.' He looked with a child's impeccable innocence into Alice's mother's eyes.

'I really had to agree,' Rosemary Armitage complained later to her husband. 'I mean, we should be glad she's so socially well inclined, I suppose. Strange, because Alice is so fastidious and he smells of drink. Quite definitely he smelled of something today.'

'Not to worry, old girl,' her husband said. 'I daresay I could have those injections. It's not too bad anyway, my allergy. Just a bit of a runny nose and sneezing. You mind it more than I do.'

'But you always make such an issue of it,' his wife said, furious at this further example of the fickleness of the male sex.

Alice went with Mr Job to collect her kitten. 'Do you have another name?' she asked him once she had the tiny orange-and-white scrap safe in the basket and under her supervision.

'Alfred. Go by the name of Alf mainly. Alfie to the chosen few.'

'I don't think that's a girl's name,' Alice said.

'But I'll call her Alfie for her middle name. Her first name is Aurora, after the Sleeping Beauty,' she explained. 'But she can be Aurora Alfie Newscastle for long.'

'You know what,' Mr Job said. 'It's a nice idea, but I would cut out the Newscastle. That's between us. We had a deal. But what it was precisely's nobody's business but yours and mine. Right, partner?'

'Right,' Alice said, squinting into the basket. 'Look, Aurora Alfie's gone to sleep.'

THE RETURN

She packed with special care for this was a special occasion: her silk nightdress, her black pearl earrings, small enough that they need not be removed in bed, the scent he liked her to wear.

She had taken a taxi from Rome's Termini station and she pursed her lips a little when the driver, assuming in her the innocence of a foreigner, took a circuitous route to stack up a bigger fare. Never mind! It was foolish to worry about money now.

Reaching the hotel, she paid the driver, registering her recognition that he had over-charged with a slight raise of her eyebrows and by insisting, in her still fluent Italian, that he carry her single suitcase inside.

The hotel, he had said to her, all that time ago, was like her, 'elegant and discreet'. They had stayed there when he took her first to Rome. Of course, the management had changed: the dark, rather poky, lobby had been transformed into a chapel of glass and light, and the old dining room, where they had never eaten, had apparently been revamped. She caught a glimpse of it as she stood at the reception desk, a dazzling vista of mirrors and chandeliers.

The elderly concierge was respectful over organising her luggage to her room. The same room, because she had described it when she booked – the one with its own small staircase leading up to it. It had also been refurbished – but not too crudely. The bathroom was now a gleam of white, with a modern shower. She didn't much care for showers. The old claw-footed bath – capacious enough for them to have shared – had been done away with. The modern replacement was only big enough for one.

She ran a bath now, and undressed, inspecting her body in the steamy mirror. It wasn't bad, considering.

Afterwards, she dressed with care, putting on her pearl earrings and the scent, then decided to take a walk before finding a suitable venue for her evening meal.

'I hope the room is all right,' Greg said. 'Is the bed big enough? I asked for a double.'

'It's lovely,' said Sophie. 'I love the private staircase. And the bed is plenty big enough,' she reassured, adding, 'I don't want to be miles away from you.'

He squeezed her arm. It had been his idea they should come to Rome. He had found the hotel through a last-minute cancellation site on the Internet. They didn't know each other well. They had met at the wedding of a friend in common and for both there was a sense of excitement, which they'd not openly shared, that their meeting might be the beginning of something beyond the ordinary.

This could be love, Sophie thought, as she undressed for a bath. He was shy with her and she sensed that he was not usually shy and that the shyness in this case meant something.

'Would you like to go for a walk before dinner?' he asked. He hadn't quite liked to watch too closely while she was dressing, though he had wanted to.

'Shall I change my shoes then?' She had put on her new heels.

'That would be a shame. I like your shoes.'

They strolled past the Pantheon, she holding on to his arm, ostensibly to keep her balance in the heels, and he translated the Latin inscription over the portico stating that Marcus Agrippa had built it in 27 BC.

'It's funny to think that people have been visiting it for over two thousand years. All those people coming and going,' Sophie said. 'Do you think they are here still?'

'How do you mean?'

'Do you think people leave a part of themselves behind in a place?'

'You mean like ghosts?'

Sophie considered this. 'I mean, do you think we rub off on places the way places rub off on us?'

A woman on her own couldn't be sure of getting attention so she inspected several restaurants. She settled finally on one of the restaurants in the piazza overlooking the Pantheon. They had gone there together, and he had explained to her how the great domed roof had been cast in concrete in one piece. It was once a temple to all the Roman gods, he had said. What ever happened to those old gods? What happened when you were no longer wanted or believed in?

The waiter was grey-haired and respectful over where she might like to sit and she was grateful for his taking trouble. She read the menu, relishing the prospect of a proper Italian meal again. It seemed a long time since she had eaten and she was hungry and looking forward to it. In the end, she settled for anchovies followed by *osso bucco* and a bottle of good Chianti. It didn't matter if she didn't drink all the bottle. This was a special occasion. She had come here to remember all that had transpired those many years ago.

They had eaten outside, then, but in a side street.

She doubted the restaurant existed now. The waiter had shown a certain tact, registering – it was hard to say quite how – his awareness that they were a couple who were not husband and wife, and that the circumstances were possibly delicate. He had tipped the waiter extra. And, in an enchanting gesture, bought her a spray of white roses from a small Italian boy with beseeching eyes. The boy had offered the flowers so winningly that she had leaned down, sweeping him to her breast and kissing his forehead. It was not the way she behaved as a rule but everyone and everything seemed beautiful that evening.

A drunk, who had been sitting quietly by the fountain in the centre of the square, suddenly began to shout wildly and throw bits of rubbish, orange peel and soggy newspaper. Presently, he moved on to plastic water bottles discarded by tourists, which he hurled with fierce imprecations and roaring yells. She watched his anger mount as the diners all round the square pointedly ignored him. She understood the rage. He had been cast aside, made to feel of no account, worthless. The drunk, furious at the lack of impact he was having, now advanced towards where she was sitting with a Coke can in his hand and chucked it with a sudden surge of savageness into the crowd of diners.

Her waiter, busy taking another order, swore under his breath, went inside the restaurant and returned with a heavily built man who walked across to the drunk and exchanged words with him.

'Oh dear,' Sophie said, watching the scene from the other side of the piazza. 'I do hope he isn't being nasty to the poor man.'

'He's drunk.'

'I know, but you know . . .' she let the implication drift.

'What?'

'Well, we might be like him, one day.'

'You could never be like him. An old drunk. Don't be silly.' He laid his hand he hoped reassuringly on hers. 'How about some Prosecco? It's cheaper than champagne but it's really quite drinkable.'

But she was still watching the small drama by the fountain. 'I could, you know. Be like him. We never know when we might be down on our luck. Anything could happen.'

He laughed a little disconcertedly. 'What sort of "anything"?'

'Oh, you know, ill health, poverty, abandonment . . . There's no telling how life may go.'

'I can't imagine anyone abandoning you, Sophie.' He looked at her with earnest eyes and her heart jumped.

'Can't you?' But at that moment the waiter arrived and they ordered, she a salad and shellfish, and he soup and the lamb.

'This is nice,' she said. The drunk had calmed down and a small boy had appeared in the gathering dusk to play the violin to them. He did not play well but none the less she gave him five euros because she was glad to be alive.

Afterwards they strolled through the cobbled streets enjoying the warmth of the evening and their own warm closeness, watching the bats flit like lost souls through the old city where so many lovers had strolled before them.

In the night he woke and felt for her body and then heard sounds from the bathroom. He stood outside the door and called, anxiously, 'Are you OK?'

'I'm being sick. It must have been the shellfish . . .'

'Oh, poor you. Do you need anything? Water? Shall I come in?'

'No, no. I'm better left. You go back to sleep, if you can.'

'But I feel badly leaving you like this, Sophie . . .'

'No, please leave me, I'll feel worse if you don't sleep too . . .'

He lay for a while worrying about her, but in the end he must have drifted off because later when he woke he felt her beside him, warm and scented. He rolled towards her. 'Darling. Are you OK?'

He felt her body turn towards his. 'Hold me. Hold me tight.'

Of course he was glad to. 'Darling Sophie.' He held her close as close. 'I am so happy that you are here with me in Rome.'

And she must have been happy too, because they made love, wildly, passionately; he did not remember ever making love like this before. Almost as if it were for the last time. And yet, they had only just begun. Or he hoped they had only just begun . . .

He woke early to the sound of the door and, thinking at first it was the maid entering prematurely, he shouted, 'We are still in bed. Room not ready yet!' Then he realised he was alone. He called out, 'Sophie?' and went to the bathroom, but it was empty save for a silk nightdress on the floor. He picked it up. The nightdress, now he looked at it, seemed oddly old fashioned, not what he would expect Sophie to wear. Though, to be honest, last night he had not noticed what she was wearing because she had turned off the light to undress. Perhaps she had changed into this after the episode of the shellfish. But where was she now?

He lay in the bed, recalling the wild lovemaking. He wished she were there beside him. He would have liked to make love to her like that again. Perhaps she had woken early and had gone out for a morning stroll?

The door opened and Sophie came into the room.

She couldn't have been out as he saw she was still in her dressing gown.

'Greg, I'm sorry. You must have been worried but I was so sick after the shellfish I couldn't sleep.' Seeing the look of puzzlement on his face she continued, 'I went to see if anyone in the hotel was up, to give me a Lomotil, or something, to soothe my stomach. The concierge was downstairs and made me peppermint tea. I think he was grateful for someone to talk to and, really, I couldn't have risked lying down. Do you know, he's been here since he was a boy? He told me all sorts of stories about the hotel.'

'What stories?' What had happened in the night? Had he dreamed that passionate exchange?

'It was the scene of a terrific drama fifty years ago. A woman killed herself. Her lover had brought her here, but it was to tell her that he was not, as she had hoped, going to leave his wife after all. He left and she was found dead in the bed from an overdose. It was the concierge's first job, and he remembers it as if it were yesterday. He couldn't remember which room, though. I hope it wasn't ours.'

'So do I.' He felt suddenly as if a goose had walked over his grave.

'Apparently, the man – he must have been quite insane to do this – brought his wife here, to the same hotel, a year later and she got sick and died, quite suddenly, in the night.'

'What did she die of?'

'The concierge didn't know. But it started rumours of the place being haunted and in the end the owners had to sell the hotel. It's been sold a few times since. It's under new management again now. Of course, he shouldn't really have told me anything . . . Greg, are you all right?'

'Sophie, what are you wearing under your dressing gown?'

'My T-shirt. Why? Don't worry, he didn't mind. I was quite respectable.'

'But you have another nightdress, no?'

'I thought I wouldn't really need one. I'm sorry last night was a bit of a frost on that front, but we've got tonight to make up for it.'

'Sophie!'

'Yes?'

'Sophie, you're – you're very pale.'

'I feel a little odd still but I expect I'll soon return to normal. Do you know, I'm so tired, I could sleep for fifty years? I think, if you don't mind, I'll sleep now . . .'

TROUBLES

I was in the process of moving my old patients' files to a new filing cabinet when I came across the file labelled 'Troubles'. I knew I would open it again eventually.

'All the troubles of the world stem from man's inability to sit still in a room,' my grandmother used to say.

She was qualified to pronounce. Both her husbands were killed after enlisting, quite needlessly, to fight in the First World War. The second was killed a year and a day after the first. They were brothers, her young husbands, and my grandmother told me she always felt guilty about the first one, Charles, because she had fancied his younger brother, Oswald, more and wondered if she had somehow managed to will Charles's death. She was not of a generation which talks about the unconscious but she intuitively understood its power. It was true that she had a great unconscious herself; I wouldn't be surprised if it had snuffed out poor Charlie.

She paid for it later though, because she really was in love with Oswald, my father's father. When he died, blown up at Vimy Ridge, my father was a four-week-old embryo in his mother's belly. I believe something blew apart then in my grandmother too. After she died, I found a silver cigarette case she had given Oswald to take to France before he became her husband and my grandfather. Engraved on it were the words, *With thou away even the birds are mute* . . . I don't think the birds sang for her much after August 1916.

When I was eighteen my grandmother gave me £100: ten big brown notes, larger than the current flimsy issue, bold as she was. When I asked her why (having been sure to thank her properly first for her generosity: you minded your manners with my grandmother) she said, 'I walked past a tramp once. He asked me for some money for a cup of tea and I was frightened. He had kind eyes.' I placed the money on a horse called Tramp and it came in at 10 to 1. That was the first time I became aware of the way the unconscious speaks. It was my first bet, too, and the money I made on betting later funded my psychoanalytic training. Of course, psychoanalysis is all about sitting still in a room.

My grandmother's words about the restlessness of men (which I learned later were really Pascal's but out of loyalty I always think of them as hers) came back to me when I met Jean Martin. He was a big, wild-looking man, of French Canadian origin, with one of those faces which look as if they have been hacked out of the Rockies, like an American president. He had my name from a psychiatrist who had heard me lecture on war and trauma.

Jean Martin sat looking out of my window, which opens on to one of the commons which make a green showing amid London's filth. Outside, on the pavement below, a child was screaming.

'You'd think someone would pick the poor little sod up.'

'It distresses you?'

'No,' was the faintly pained answer. 'Why d'you think it would?'

Well, that was a start. One doesn't usually strike such a rich seam so soon: anger, pain, and a defensive untruth all in an opening couple of remarks.

'I was wondering if maybe you felt sorry for the child?'

A shrug. He was beaten, or something, as a kid, I thought.

My patient stared moodily out at the green and then, still looking out of the window dropped the first of what I came to recognise as his kind of red-herring.

241

'Have you ever been in a helicopter?'

There are all kinds of reasons why I like my job but perhaps the easiest to explain is its variety. In no other profession does one have the opportunity to discuss such a range of topics. But I could think of no one before who had introduced helicopters.

'No,' I said.

That is not what we were trained to say. We were trained to reveal nothing of ourselves, to say, 'What is it about helicopters that . . .?' Never reveal one's personal preferences or experience, is the canonical position. But I have a different view. The truth has advantages. It's more consistent. It shall set ye free, as a not inconsiderable healer once said; and although he was speaking of the larger truth that one must learn to tell oneself, he might have agreed that one can make a start by telling truths to others. So I see no harm in meeting questions with truthful answers.

'You should,' he said, 'it's good for the imagination.'

I could see this might be true. All that curving and cutting through the air must act as a powerful release. 'Tell me about it,' I said, and sat back. I guessed I was about to be enlightened.

He was a consultant engineer but, he explained, he had been taught to fly years before. Although he was vague about the circumstances, I gathered that there had been some military connection.

Whatever the reason, the accomplishment had since become an enthusiasm: his craggy face shone with his account of mountain flying.

When people tell us their stories, we allow our minds to wander a pace above, or below (I never quite know where to locate it) their drift. So we track what is being said as it were from a moving position. It struck me now, listening to what Jean Martin was saying, that this position is very like a helicopter's tracking flight. One has to fly in and out of some odd places in the mind.

And it prompted me to say, 'It reminds me a little of what I do.'

At that point the child started up again and this time he said, 'For Christ's sake, why don't they pick it up?'

'What would you do with him?' I asked. I wasn't having any truck with that 'it': it was pretty clear whom we were talking about.

But either he wasn't ready or my timing was out. 'I don't know,' he said. 'How d'you mean, it's like what you do?'

The first meeting is everything. You do all the essential work in the first meeting and the rest is putting it in its place. It's the same with a love affair: when you meet someone and fall in love, you know all there is to know about them. Then you forget, wishing reality to be otherwise. After a while you see the way things are, as if for the first time (you forget you've known it all along) and that's when the hard work has to start. Once that has set in, love – real love, I mean – has a chance. It is not so different with patients except, unlike a love affair, you shouldn't forget what it is that needs to be granted another's blessing, or charity, or forgiveness. It is your business to notice that.

I watched Jean Martin shifting about in the chair, as he talked about his helicopter flying, and my grandmother's maxim came into my mind. What troubles has this man been caught up in? I wondered. And what is it caused the restlessness?

He left after fifty minutes were up and I still did not know why he had come to consult me. But I knew what I needed to know: whatever was haunting him was connected to an inability to sit still in a room.

I was right about the child. It took some time for the full story to emerge but it was a miserable tale of physical and emotional violence. It had bred in him a combination of resentment and idealisation, a tough mix to live with. There were repeated examples of unnecessary courage, pointless generosity, over enthusiasm for this person or that position, followed by a biting of the hand that fed or loved him. He idealised me: it was obvious from the start he would.

The first time a patient fell in love with me I became alarmed. Even with all the preparatory theoretical training, nothing quite prepares you for the reality of the experience. It is unlike unrequited love in ordinary life because the love a patient feels for you is not unrequited: but the love with which one answers is of a different quality. But it is still love – which can be bewildering. 'It is part of what we must suffer,' my old supervisor said. 'Stop fussing about it. It goes with this job. Accept it. It won't last.' Later I saw it as not unlike the love of one's children – only ours for a space.

When Jean Martin fell 'in love' with me he fell very hard. I watched it happen almost before my eyes and I wanted to say then, 'It's all right. You'll get over it. One day you will see my real face again and I will seem merely a friendly middle-aged woman who does not mind what you say to her.'

I remember the day it happened because I had had a row with my husband. Sometimes I work better when I am having a row – it sharpens my attention. I was wearing a dress I like, a blue dress with a bias in the cut. I had put it on so that my husband would be aware of what he might miss if I walked out on him.

Jean Martin came into the room and sat down in the chair opposite. For once he didn't shift his buttocks about in his usual restless way. He sat upright looking dead at me. Then he said, 'Your dress is the colour of the sky. I shall see you in it when I fly.'

I didn't reply. I just waited, noting that he had made a small poem with his words.

'There's no point, is there?' he said then.

I guessed what he had in mind but all I said was 'I suppose that depends what you mean by "point".'

'You're married, aren't you? You have a husband.'

'Yes,' I said. 'I am married. I have a husband.'

'I love you,' he said. He said it without rancour.

'Yes,' I said. And waited.

We sat awhile in silence. I wondered whether he had been brought to his declaration by some invisible communication of the row I was having with my husband.

'It's pointless asking if you love me back?'

'There's every point,' I said, 'but the kind of way I may love you may not seem very satisfactory to you.' Long ago a clever tutor said to me, 'You shouldn't have affairs with your patients. It may or may not hurt them but it will certainly hurt you.' I extend this prohibition to platonic love affairs.

There was silence. Then Jean Martin left the room. After a bit, I heard his tread coming back up the stairs. It was still his session time so I let him in again and returned to my chair and sat there, waiting to see what he would say. Or not say.

'Don't talk about me, will you?' he said. 'I mean not to your husband.'

*　*　*

Jean Martin showed no sign of ringing me in the night, or of hanging around our house. He didn't sit all day on the flight of steps which lead up to our Richmond home or overwhelm me with letters, or interrupt the process of enquiry we were engaged in together with sighs or mournful asides. Indeed, he was tactful with his feelings – only murmuring from time to time, 'You won't say anything, will you?'

The row with my husband had long since blown over and we were out together one day in Richmond Park. I had been racing our dog, Mishkin, and had slipped, fallen and twisted my foot. Bill, who is quintessentially a rational man, was struggling to be kind when he plainly thought that what I had done was daft and my own fault. I had mud on my knees and on my skirt and my face was flushed with the cold and the running and perhaps also with some anger. (Bill could make me feel silly when I didn't act my age.)

I was sitting on a bench with my boot off, massaging my ankle when someone approached and said, 'Can I be of assistance?' It was Jean Martin.

Bill was about to utter some polite rejoinder when I saw him pause. Just for a second he seemed – what was it? Not quite his usual urbane self? No. More than usually his urbane self, that's what it was. To Jean Martin he said, 'Thanks, old man, she's with me. She'll be fine.'

Sometimes, if one is lucky, one catches these moments as they occur, like a kingfisher flashing in front of the eyes before one has had time to register it. As I observed that pared-down pause between the two men, who had together bent their heads towards my injured foot, I witnessed something. They knew each other. More than that, they had a history.

'Nice of that chap,' Bill said as he escorted me to the Volvo.

'Mmm,' I said. I didn't reveal that I knew him.

On the morning we met next, Jean Martin made no mention of the Richmond Park encounter. He sat with his usual restlessness describing aspects of his adolescence. Taking my cue from his silence I too said nothing. There was nothing remarkable in what he told me that morning, save that, unusually, I was bored, and boredom is a clue. Generally, it means there is something artificial in whatever is being said. I was so bored that at several moments I found my eyelids weighing and a longing for sleep creeping over me. So it was a jolt when he said, 'I shan't be coming any more.'

'Ah,' I said, playing for time. I was genuinely surprised. And then, because it seemed best to become blunt, 'Why?'

But I had guessed the answer. It was Bill.

I could not exactly define the moment when I first suspected that what Bill did at the Foreign

Office was not entirely straightforward. He was older than me by ten years and had been up at Cambridge at the period when recruitment to MI5 was still persuasive. His position, I knew, had taken him, in the days before our marriage, on various lengthy trips abroad. It's my job to piece together bits of lives to make a whole so it is hardly surprising that I pieced together Bill's.

'You're a spy, aren't you, or were, anyway,' I said one Sunday over breakfast. The thought had come to me while we had been making love that morning.

'Don't be absurd,' Bill said. But his hand carrying the cup to his lip made just a fractional pause. It was the same kind of pause I witnessed in him when, twenty years later, Jean Martin had come upon us in Richmond Park.

Now, sitting in my consulting room, with the sparrows rowdily chatting in the eaves, Jean Martin did not pause but said, 'Because it may be dangerous if I stay.'

I knew he hoped I would suppose he was referring to his feelings for me but what struck me was the directness with which he spoke. His words, although ambiguous, were not deceitful. By now, I was definitely wide awake.

'For whom?' I asked. 'Dangerous for whom?'

He didn't answer this but he said something startling. 'I know, knew, your husband.'

'Yes, I had gathered.' This was risky but it felt right.

'But not from him?' Anxious now.

'No,' I agreed. 'Not from him.' Which of course gave a good deal away.

'So then,' he said, as if that were explanation enough.

'So?' I said. 'What has my husband to do with what happens here?'

At this he looked at me with his rather round blue-grey eyes as if I were an idiot or something. But he said nothing. So I pressed on.

'If you and my husband have a past connection then nothing you tell me about it will be passed on to him. Or to anyone – of course,' I added, a shade defensively.

'I know that,' Jean Martin said. He sat and did something with his hands which was almost twiddling his thumbs. Then he said, 'I've done things, your husband has done things, which only we know about. I can't, you see . . .'

He stopped short so I finished for him. 'Tell me?'

'I can't tell you,' he agreed. And then repeated what he'd said before. 'It would be dangerous.'

'For you?' Still he sat there. 'For Bill? For my husband.' Silence. 'You mean it might be dangerous for me?'

He shrugged but his eyes gave him away.

'You are protecting me?'

250

'Maybe,' he agreed.

There is a saying of the old French wizard Lacon: when the patient comes, they speak directly but not of the secret; then they speak of the secret, but not directly; when they speak directly of the secret they are free to go. For much of the time, let me add, no one is in possession of the secret.

We sat a little longer in silence but this time neither of us broke it. He left the room to reappear, seconds later, in the doorway as he had the very first time we had met.

'Don't tell your husband about this, will you?'

'I won't,' I said. 'You are quite safe.'

I felt perturbed as I made my slow way home through traffic that night. I didn't imagine for a second I was in danger from Bill, but it is impossible not to be moved by another's impossible love, the more so if it is directed at oneself. Besides I liked Jean Martin. Patients don't appreciate this but we have idiosyncrasies, likes and dislikes, too. I liked him and I felt pity for him. But I now see there was more. If I had had to answer before the Recording Angel I would have been forced to say that a part of me wished I had another life in which I might reciprocate his feelings. There was then no question of it in this life. I was bound to Bill by ties I had never tried to analyse.

Over the next week or so I waited for Jean Martin

at his usual time and finally when he did not appear I rang him. But the number he had given me was either false or the phone had been disconnected. He had paid my bills on demand so although I had an address he had also given me I was doubtful that any letter would reach him. Some months passed and something about Bill began to alarm me, so hard to put my finger on that I would almost have said my perception was faulty were it not for the events that followed. It wasn't that he became obviously preoccupied or disturbed. In every way he spoke and acted as he had always done. It was just this sense of a slight ruffling behind his habitual calm which aggravated it. Much as he had become so super cool that time I twisted my foot in Richmond Park. But I never enquired what the matter might be. That was my weakness with Bill. I sat all day silently or overtly making enquiries and it was restful not to have to bother at home. Besides, I knew it would have been useless. He wouldn't have levelled with me. Our intimacy was not of that kind.

One evening, he didn't come home. I wasn't especially worried since occasionally he would do this. It was always some unexpected work thing and it wasn't unusual for him not to ring to let me know. Bill was like that. Secretive. But as I say, I had enough of other people's secrets concealed within me not to bother about Bill's.

It was almost midnight when the phone rang. I had fallen asleep and was not immediately sure where I was or what time of day it was so I must have sounded strange. I felt sure, though, it was Bill.

'Darling,' I said, 'where ever are you? What's going on?' and there was a long silence at the other end of the phone.

Then someone said, 'I am so sorry' and put the phone down.

When the police arrived the following day, I had just returned from work and had my shoes off and was watching the news. They told me Bill had been found dead somewhere in Dorset, a part of the country to which he had no known reason to travel. It appeared he had been alone, had somehow slipped and in the fall his neck had been broken. A colleague reported that Bill had said he had a luncheon date and had not returned. Although there was no evidence of any lunch appointment in his diary, the police said they were treating the death as accidental.

What weighed on me most was that I could never know what past knot it was between those two men that had led to the death of one of them, for I knew at once and with every fibre of my being that this was no accident. I had lived with Bill for twenty-one years and yet – and this is the weirdest thing – of the two men I would say I knew Jean

Martin better. For one thing he had told me of his own volition what Bill had never divulged. Which is how I came to see that it was no accident that we met him that day in Richmond Park. He must have been shadowing me, using whatever his past skills had taught him to watch over me. It was chance (or maybe fate?) that Bill turned out to be my husband. This is also why I know that it was Bill who must have instigated the violence against Jean and that Jean had killed Bill purely in self-defence. Whatever shadow loomed from their shared past Jean would never have killed a man who was important to me.

I never saw Jean Martin again but I have wondered whether I might have been wrong about his love. It might have been the kind that sticks. Which might have meant more than a life saved had my husband only learned how to sit still in a room.

THE FALL OF A SPARROW

'I think I may die,' Rebecca said aloud one morning. She did not mean she intended to kill herself. Only that things seemed suddenly more than she felt she could bear. It was to a single sparrow out on her small, slightly dingy balcony, that, quite undramatically, she addressed these words.

Years ago, Rebecca had fallen in love with Frank. Frank Butler was her university tutor, who taught the class on Romantic poetry which Rebecca had attended, as a mature student, when she first moved to London. The class had read Keats, on whom Rebecca had written an essay, commenting on the poet's untimely death, which had found favour with her tutor.

Frank was older than Rebecca, married with a young family. It was not he but Rebecca who had insisted that he mustn't leave his wife until the children were old enough. He had been the one who had wanted to fly off with her. 'You will feel guilty,' she had told him. 'And regret it. And then you will regret me, and that I would mind.'

They had waited; but as anyone who has been in this situation discovers, children are never 'old enough' for their parents to split up safely. And, however irksome, the claims of marital responsibility tend to foreclose over time.

After ten years, Rebecca asked, tactfully, whether or not Frank envisaged their ever moving in together. He had answered not exactly shiftily but it was impossible not to register the lack of the first fine careless protestations. During the early years of knowing Frank Rebecca had turned down other promising alliances. One in particular, Tim Robbins, who had emigrated to South Africa, she thought of at this point. She even went so far as to email him. Tim replied with news of his family, explaining that his wife, a former ballet dancer, was training to be a doctor. Rebecca deleted the pictures of the blue swimming pool and laughing children and did not repeat this experiment.

By the time the Butler children were at university, Rebecca felt the moment had arrived for a straight talk with Frank. Samantha, Frank's daughter, had recovered from the anorexia which had set her back during her first year, and Keir was well on his way to a doctorate in chemical engineering. 'Are we ever going to live together?' she asked one afternoon.

They were in bed having made love. The love-making was more of a ritual by now. But perhaps it is sentimental to expect passions to retain their initial force. 'I don't know,' Frank had said, with unusual candour.

This was the first time any doubt on this matter had ever been voiced and Rebecca's chest tightened. 'Don't you love me any more?' she asked, and cursed herself. She knew better than to ask this question. But like it or not, it is not always our 'better' selves who speak for us.

'Of course I do,' Frank said, in something like his old tone.

'Not enough to live with me though?' She had got her voice back under control.

'I don't know,' he said again. 'It's not that I don't love you.'

'You love Evelyn more?'

He frowned, and again she felt sorry for him. She rarely pushed, and she was aware that this was a crucial element in her appeal. 'Not the way I love you. But where would she go if I left her?'

Rebecca did not ask: 'Where will I go if you and I part?' She got out of bed and put on her dressing gown and went to wash up the lunch. When he came to say goodbye she was in the kitchen staring out of the window of her high mansion flat.

'What are you thinking?'

'I was wishing I was a bird,' she said, watching a solitary seagull which had strayed inland.

'So you could fly away from me?'

'So at least I could fly somewhere.'

That autumn, the *season of mists and mellow fruitfulness,* as he had once written to her on a postcard, Frank explained he was taking Evelyn to Venice for their twenty-fifth wedding anniversary. Venice was where he and Rebecca had always planned to go, when they were free. Rebecca found the card which for all those years had been stuck in her volume of Keats to mark the famous ode – a drawing of a naked woman whose torso Frank had flatteringly compared to hers – drank most of a bottle of gin and wrote a letter. She carried it around in her bag for three days before finally dropping it into the post box.

Frank didn't ring when he returned but then she had particularly asked that he shouldn't. Nevertheless, very few of us really want even our most ardently phrased requests obeyed. After waiting by the phone all weekend, she woke on the Monday, looked out the card and then tore it into little bits and dropped it over the balcony outside her flat. She delivered her bleak pronouncement to a sparrow which had flown down and perched on the balcony rail beside her. 'I think I may die,' she had said.

Keats had liked sparrows. *If a sparrow come before my window, I take part in its existence and pick about the gravel,* he had written. It was the same letter where he had asserted, *I am certain of nothing but the holiness of the heart's affections.* Keats had brought her into this hopeless situation. But he died in pain believing he was unloved.

On an impulse, Rebecca booked a holiday in Rome.

It was raining when she arrived at the sequestered so-called Protestant Cemetery just outside a remainder of the old walls of ancient Rome. She wandered along the grassy paths in the rain-dark light till she found what she was looking for, Keats's gravestone on which was carved his own forlorn epitaph: *Here lies One Whose Name was writ in Water.* The words he wrote and requested be his final memorial just before he died far from home, and his beloved, in humble lodgings on the Spanish Steps.

She stood there, astonished that there was nothing more to indicate the abiding genius of the twenty-seven-year-old poet who believed that his poems would be as ephemeral as his life.

The rain had begun to fall more heavily when she heard a voice.

'You will catch cold.' A pale young man had apparently followed her to the graveside. 'Come under the tree.'

He gestured towards a tall pine and they stood together, he holding his coat over their heads. He was smaller than Rebecca and slighter, so that to cover her head he had to stretch. His coat was rather worn and of an old-fashioned cloth and cut.

'Why have you come here?' he asked. He looked as if he might have suffered a long illness.

'I saw a sparrow,' she said. 'It made me think of Keats.'

'You like Keats?' His dark eyes in his thin face were brightly enquiring.

'He liked sparrows. He wrote to a friend once, *If a sparrow come before my window, I take part in its existence and pick about the gravel.*'

'Yes,' the pale young man agreed. 'You are right. He did love birds.'

'There aren't many sparrows left in London these days. I thought how he might have minded.'

'So you came here?'

'I wanted to die,' she said. 'So I came here.'

'Oh, you mustn't die,' he said. And he looked at her with such urgency in his eyes that she had to look away. 'Believe me. No one is worth dying for.'

Side by side they stood, so close that she felt the shadow of his breath on her cold cheek. As the rain eased, a sparrow fluttered down and perched delicately on the tombstone.

'Look,' she whispered to her companion. Turning to him, she found there was no one beside her but the pine tree and the only breath a faint stirring of wind.